10549329

Also by Leone Sperling

Coins for the Ferryman

Mother's Day

Oasis

What about love?

Book of Life

Jamie longs for love and acceptance. A debilitating childhood illness has left him with physical disabilities but he believes that some day someone will look beneath the surface, see his inner worth and love him for his true self. Despite constant rejection he continues to see every girl who crosses his path as the potential answer to his search for a loving life companion.

As he endeavours to carve out a creative life for himself his great need for acceptance and love often alienates those around him. Leone Sperling's JAMIE is a poignant and moving tale of a young man's search for love and understanding.

JAMIE

A novel by Leone Sperling

Cover design and typeset by Green Avenue Design.

Published by Cilento Publishing, Australia.

ISBN: 978-0-9925602-0-1

CHAPTER 1

Walter Liebler was a man who could not tolerate imperfection. That was one reason why he felt irritated by his wife. He knew that Elizabeth could not help having thick ankles. A childhood disease had caused a thickening of the bones, a fact that marred her in his eyes. He looked at her as he crept into the dimly lit hospital room. High forehead, patrician nose, faded blonde hair swept off her face into a tight, neat, housewifely bun at the back of her head. Her navy, button-up, shirt-maker dress looked crumpled from the hours spent sitting beside Jamie's bed. It was 9 p.m. and she'd been there all day. When she became aware of Walter's presence, Elizabeth could not help eyeing him with disapproval.

'Couldn't you get here any earlier?'

'You know how it is. They were short staffed at Elizabeth Bay. I had to sort things out.' Walter owned three busy coffee lounges and often worked a seventy hour week.

'Jamie longed to see you. He kept asking, "When's Daddy coming?" and I kept saying, "Soon. He'll be here soon." And now it's too late,' she cried. 'They gave him his sleeping pills half an hour ago.'

'I'm sorry.' And he was indeed sorry. He did not know how to explain to Elizabeth that witnessing ten-year-old Jamie's pain was so distressing that he could only bear it for a few moments at a time. He admired Elizabeth for being able to spend day after day with their son because he could not, personally, understand how such a thing was possible. Her implied criticism of his failure to be more attentive to Jamie upset him but because he had so much respect for Elizabeth's ability to cope with this appalling situation he did not want to do anything to upset her. 'How high was his temperature today?'

'Still high,' replied Elizabeth. 'Up to 105 degrees at times. Headache. Pains in the knees and ankles. Arms and shoulders aching.'

'And did they tell you anything today? These marvellous doctors of yours at this high-class private hospital?' Walter's irritation with Elizabeth gave way to an anger that he could not suppress. 'Are they any closer to diagnosing this mystery disease your son is suffering from?'

'They still don't know what's wrong with him,' she said.

'Two weeks? And they still don't know? I want him moved to the Children's Hospital. And I want him moved tomorrow,' Walter insisted.

'We've been through this before, Walter. Dr Bradley and his associates are respected children's specialists. Jamie is in the best possible hands.'

'One more week, Elizabeth. That's all I'll give them. Now get your things. I'll drive you home.'

'Aren't you coming home?'

'I've got things to do,' said Walter and they had nothing more to say to each other as he drove her to their unpretentious, red-bricked, comfortable cottage in the quiet backstreets of Chatswood.

It was a half hour drive to Zelda's apartment and that's where Walter was going now. Zelda. His mistress. Dark-haired, bold, voluptuous, sensuous. Full of life and laughter. Always ready for love-making. Her firm-fleshed thighs eager to enclose him, drawing him into the wondrous depths of her desire. He couldn't get enough of her.

How could a man like Walter have married a woman like Elizabeth? And stayed married to her for twelve years? These were questions that thirty-five year old Walter asked himself every day.

Of course the answers lay in the past but Walter wanted to focus on the future and he did not see how the future could be tolerated if he remained married to Elizabeth. And yet, poor Elizabeth was not to blame. He felt sorry for her. That was the problem. And because he pitied her he found it difficult to abandon her. And then, of course, there was Jamie.

Walter had come to Australia in 1933, at the age of eighteen, and he still cringed when he recalled how naive he had been. His uncle had brought him out as a sponsored migrant. His own father, who had been a lawyer, had died when Walter was twelve and his Australian uncle had felt obliged to send money to keep the boy in school. Naturally, when he arrived in Australia, he believed his education would continue. How shocked he had been to find that the Australian branch of his family were not in a financial position to send their own children to university, let alone a nephew fresh from Europe. He was expected, like everyone else, to work in the family clothing factory and he was, moreover, expected to be grateful.

And that wasn't the only shock. His own parents had been tolerant, educated, assimilated, cosmopolitan Jews but his Australian relatives were narrow-minded, bigoted, prejudiced and tightly locked into a closed, self-imposed, Jewish ghetto. And they expected Walter to live his life within their prescribed boundaries. When they took him out for breakfast, on his first Sunday in Australia, he made a bad impression by ordering bacon with his eggs. His transgressions soon progressed from the trivial to the unforgivable. Walter was exuberant, gregarious and so intoxicated by the opportunities Sydney offered that he made friends outside of the Jewish community. This was viewed as intolerable by his family. He was tall, dark, solidly built and loved sports of all kinds. He surfed at Sydney beaches, joined a tennis club and went climbing in the Blue Mountains. He was not handsome but his joy of life was so infectious that girls were captivated and easily won. Rumours of his licentious behaviour were quickly reported to Walter's uncle who told him that he had become a pariah. If he didn't change his ways he would be out of a job and he could not expect to continue living in his uncle's house if he was going to behave in such an immoral fashion.

Walter did not wait to be thrown out. He left of his own accord. He rented a small bachelor flat at Kings Cross where he could enjoy making love to the large number of girls who were eager to share his bed. He found employment as a waiter in a well-established city restaurant. Within a few months he had made himself indispensable to the proprietor and was soon managing the place. He worked hard and saved his money. By the time he met Elizabeth, five years later, he was almost ready to go into business for himself. In 1938, Sydney lacked continental-style coffee lounges and Walter could see that great opportunities lay in that direction. At twenty-three Walter was very determined to prove to his uncle that he could succeed alone. He was equally determined to continue living his own life on his own terms.

Walter met Elizabeth at a Saturday night dance at the Tro-cadero. He was not sexually attracted to her but her tall, cool elegance caught his eye and he asked her to dance. She had recently come to Sydney from Tasmania and Walter offered to take her out and show her around.

Elizabeth was pure and innocent and good. There was a sweetness about her face that he found appealing. She was a virgin and intended to remain that way until she married. They held hands and exchanged perfunctory, passionless kisses but she would not allow any closer physical contact. Nor did he seek anything more because, quite honestly, she failed to arouse his passion. Walter was, however, pleased to be seen with her. There was something deeply satisfying in the fact that this sophisticated, well-bred girl, of pedigreed English stock, chose to walk down the street holding the hand of a somewhat swarthy, immigrant boy with a very obvious foreign accent.

Her body was slender with a tiny waist and her breasts and hips created agreeable, adequate, well-proportioned curves. He did not notice her ankles until the first time he took her to Bondi Beach for a swim. As she took off her dress he looked at her neat figure with admiration but when they stretched out on their beach towels his eyes travelled down her legs and stopped in disappointment when they reached her ankles. He looked away and gazed out to sea.

'I had osteomyelitis when I was fourteen,' said Elizabeth. 'I'm embarrassed when I come to the beach because the illness has left me with thickened ankles. Perhaps other people don't notice them as much as I think they do. I hope you don't mind.'

'Of course not,' said Walter. 'Come on, let's go in for a swim.' But he did mind. He minded very much and he became obsessed with her imperfection. Whenever he was with her he tried to avoid looking at her legs but his eyes seemed to be compulsively drawn to them and every time his glance moved downwards to her ankles he felt both distaste and displeasure.

He continued to spend a considerable amount of his time with Elizabeth and she began to regard him as her boyfriend.

He did not mind her viewing him in this way. Indeed, he was flattered although he had no intention of giving up his other girlfriends and continued to enjoy his sexual romps with willing bedfellows. Elizabeth, of course, knew nothing about his sexual life.

Elizabeth was the same age as Walter, twenty-three, and it was imperative for her to find a husband. She entrusted Walter with the knowledge of the tragedy of her life. Her own sister had stolen Elizabeth's boyfriend away from her and married him. So devastating had this event proved to be that she had fled Tasmania and come to Sydney. She still felt betrayed, wronged, injured and outraged. The only way she could recover self-esteem was by finding a husband. If she could bring a boyfriend back to Tasmania, if she could show her family that she'd found a man willing and eager to marry her, then perhaps she could comfortably resume her place in her family's social world. And she thought that Walter would be willing to take on that role because she offered something that he did not have. What she offered was a step up into a higher class of society. He would not have been able to make that transition on his own.

She put him to the test. She told Walter that she would leave him and go back to Tasmania if he didn't marry her. Her proposal terrified him and he told her the truth, that although he was very fond of her he did not feel ready for marriage. He could not imagine giving up all those other girlfriends. His refusal was a blow to Elizabeth's fragile self-esteem and she returned to her family in tears.

Walter was surprised to find that he missed her. That sweet face, with its shy and gentle smile, invaded his consciousness and stole into his dreams. He decided to follow her. He had a few weeks' annual holidays due. He would go to Tasmania and visit her and, at the same time, he'd be able to indulge his passion for bush walking and mountain climbing.

Elizabeth's parents were apprehensive at first but Walter's ability to charm almost everyone he met soon won him their acceptance. Her father was heartened by the fact that Walter did not appear to come from European peasant stock. After all, his father had been a lawyer and two of his uncles, who had migrated to America, were doctors. They were impressed when Walter told them that he had completed arrangements for a bank loan and intended to go into business for himself within the next few months.

Walter did not want to waste too much time in winning the approval of Elizabeth's family. He wanted to get out into those marvellous Tasmanian mountains and planned a week long, adventurous, camping holiday. Naturally, he expected Elizabeth to accompany him but Elizabeth's mother was adamant - no marriage, no camping trip.

This put Walter in an awkward situation. He felt no more ready for marriage than when Elizabeth had first suggested it but her family seemed to assume that he would not have followed her to Tasmania if he hadn't been serious about her. And Walter was, in many ways, an honourable young man. When he thought of Elizabeth's goodness and innocence, he was reminded of the goodness and innocence of his own mother, whom he adored. He found himself agreeing to the marriage and was quite surprised when Elizabeth's parents suggested a swift, no-frills, registry office wedding. Within a few days Walter was married to Elizabeth and they were off on their honeymoon camping holiday. Before he left, Walter sent a letter to his mother, telling her that he had married a woman who was just like her. 'Surely, Mother,' he wrote, 'you must know that I could never marry anyone who was not like you.'

In theory, Walter did believe that marriage was sacrosanct, that loyalty, fidelity and respect for one's wife were values to be admired. He had been brought up to honour family duty and responsibility and he did not think that Elizabeth and her parents had trapped him into marriage. He could see that his own behaviour had led to certain expectations and because he was a well brought-up young man, he had felt obliged to fulfil those expectations. However, he did not want a wife and he did not want the obligation of looking after a family so that he found it impossible to put his theoretical view of marriage into practice.

It was not easy for either of them. Having lost her boyfriend to her sister, Elizabeth was very jealous of her husband. She wanted him to be with her all the time and he found her possessiveness suffocating. Although she constantly told him how much she loved him, there was no passion to her love-making and he longed for the bodies of the wild, carefree girlfriends he had enjoyed before the marriage. The fights began almost immediately. They played tennis with friends one night a week and Elizabeth always found fault with Walter's behaviour.

'You kept looking at Esther. Every time she served the ball you were watching her skirt ride up over her pants!'

'I wasn't the only man there who noticed what terrific legs she's got,' said Walter.

'She's got terrific legs and my legs are ugly. That's what you mean, isn't it?' cried Elizabeth.

'I didn't say that,' said Walter.

'And what about Mary? What were you doing with her when you both went into the shed? You were in there for ten minutes.'

'Talking. Just talking.'

'You were flirting with Mary. I saw you. Everyone saw you. You can't do that any more. You're my husband.'

Elizabeth thought that Walter was always looking at other women and there was certainly an element of truth in this belief. Every time he was out of her sight, she imagined that he was flirting with or sleeping with other women. Walter found this jealousy flattering. He provoked it and played upon it to satisfy his own ego. He was especially cruel at balls and dances. He would leave Elizabeth to fend for herself and deliberately choose brassy, sexy women as dancing partners. How threatening it must have been to her to witness his attraction to women that she regarded as vulgar, women who were so different from herself.

When he opened the coffee lounge in Elizabeth Bay, he had to work very hard to establish his new business. Hours were long and he inevitably worked late into the night. He would come home to a battery of questions. 'Where have you been? Who did you meet? Who did you take out to dinner? Who did you sleep with?'

There was, at first, no truth to these accusations but Elizabeth's jealousy developed so rapidly into paranoia that Walter found no point in defending himself. Very soon he found no point in remaining faithful to her. He might as well do the things he was accused of doing. He was, however, discreet in his affairs. The hours at the coffee shop did make infidelity possible but his staff were very loyal and when Elizabeth rang up to check on him, they would give her a very plausible excuse for his absence. Within six months Walter knew that, as far as he was concerned, the marriage was not just a mistake but a failure.

Elizabeth spent her days in fevered anguish, torturing herself with scenarios of Walter's imagined infidelities. She could not understand why he behaved in such a way. He was her husband, wasn't he? And she was a good and loving wife. Surely that was all that was necessary. She tried, in her own mind, to make excuses for him. Walter was very young. In time he would settle down. She must be calm and patient. They would have children. He would love those children and then he would conform to the role of husband and father that she envisioned for him.

When Elizabeth became pregnant she was ecstatic and Walter was appalled. She saw pregnancy as the means to cementing the bonds of their marriage and he saw it as another step towards his own imprisonment. When Elizabeth began to bleed, late one Sunday afternoon, he dutifully took her to the hospital but then went off to the coffee lounge. When the bleeding resulted in a miscarriage he simply could not understand the reason for her hysteria.

When she fell pregnant again, a few months later, Walter tried to be more accepting of the situation. He did not stop sleeping with other women and he did not work fewer hours because of Elizabeth's pregnancy but he did try to avoid fights and confrontations. Although Walter hated being married to Elizabeth and could not help behaving in ways that would hurt her, he did not, at this stage, contemplate leaving her. Although Elizabeth annoyed him, he continued to see her as blameless. It was not her fault that he could not love her. At this point of time he tried to be philosophical about his marriage. Some marriages were happy and some were not. That was life. You simply had to learn to live with the situation you found yourself in.

Elizabeth did not lose this baby but so much depended on keeping it that she was sick and anxious for several months. She saw the pregnancy as the most momentous event in her life but in fact, on the broader world stage, a far more important event was taking place. World War II broke out some months before Jamie's birth and this was to have repercussions on Elizabeth's life that she could not have foreseen. Walter, luckily, could read the signs of the times and realised that his adored mother, his beloved older sister, Miriam, and her husband, Jacob, would not be safe if they remained in Europe. His mother did not meet the Australian requirements for immigration but she was allowed to join members of her family in America. Walter managed to obtain Australian visas for Miriam and Jacob. They were living in Prague at the time and later told of sitting huddled together on the bed of a hotel room, listening to the Germans march into Prague and wondering if they would ever be able to get away. Fortunately, at that initial stage of the war, the Germans were glad to get rid of any Jews who had exit visas and boat tickets and even supervised their embarkation. A German official stamped Miriam's passport and asked her where she was going.

'To Australia,' she replied.

'Watch out for the sharks there,' said the German officer. Then he laughed and sneered at her, 'You won't have to worry. Even a shark wouldn't touch a Jew.'

When Miriam and Jacob arrived in Australia, Walter saw it as his duty to sustain and support them until they could establish themselves in Australia. Elizabeth did not like the fact that Walter's hard-earned money was spent on his sister and her husband and she resented the time and energy that he devoted to their welfare. Walter could understand her jealousy of his extra-marital affairs but when she extended her attack to the help he gave to his family he was furious. How could she complain? How could she be so jealous? How could she be so small-minded, so mean-spirited? They were refugees. They were obviously in need of help. They were family. The only thing that saved Elizabeth from the full force of his anger was the fact that his sister, Miriam, was so obviously delighted to learn that Walter was to become a father.

The birth was long and painful but Jamie brought a momentary euphoria. Elizabeth felt her status rise in her husband's estimation as he responded to the birth of a son with pride and love. The baby was strong and healthy, with no observable imperfections and when Walter first looked at him he knew that Jamie would, forever, be his own very special responsibility.

A few weeks after the birth, however, Jacob, who had been an officer in the Czech army, made the extraordinary decision to return to Europe and rejoin his regiment. Walter responded to this by informing Elizabeth that they were going to move to a duplex that he had arranged to rent in Artarmon. Miriam would live upstairs and he and Elizabeth and Jamie would live downstairs.

Elizabeth was furious. 'I don't want to have your sister living with us!'

'She won't be living with us. She'll be living upstairs,' said Walter.

'You have your own family to look after now - a child. You shouldn't be spending money on your sister. You should be thinking of providing for our future - mine and Jamie's,' said Elizabeth.

'Miriam's working. She's earning money. I'll only be helping her a little bit with the rent. I want her close to me so that I can look after her while Jacob's away. How can you be so jealous? She's my sister!'

But there was good reason for Elizabeth's jealousy. Walter spent a great deal of time with Miriam. He took her to concerts, to the theatre, out for dinner. He left poor Elizabeth at home, house-bound, breast feeding, attending to the demanding needs of a newborn baby. Elizabeth was so exhausted, so weepy and so angry with him that he spent as little time as possible at home. His strong sense of responsibility for Jamie, in the early months of his son's life, did not extend any further than the provision of more than adequate financial support. He had no understanding at all of Elizabeth's situation. What was wrong with her? She'd wanted to be a mother and now she did nothing but complain. Couldn't she ever be satisfied?

By the time Jamie was three months old, Walter decided he couldn't stand it any longer. The baby was healthy but cried vigorously throughout the night and Walter couldn't get any sleep. Elizabeth never stopped nagging and she constantly made the accusation that his sister was undermining the marriage. This culminated in what Walter saw as Elizabeth's irrational hysteria over the fact that Miriam, quite innocently, had bought herself a dress that was a replica of one that Elizabeth owned.

'Look what she's doing,' screamed Elizabeth. 'Can't you see what she's doing to me? Now she even thinks she can take over from me by wearing a dress that's exactly like mine! She's trying to destroy our marriage. There was nothing wrong with our relationship until she came here. Now she's stealing you away from me.'

Walter needed a break so he took his sister away with him to the Hydro Majestic Hotel in Medlow Bath for the weekend. While they were there he told Miriam that he would have to leave Elizabeth.

'But you can't do that,' said Miriam. 'Walter, you have a child. What would our mother say?'

And mother was, indeed, a major consideration. America had not yet entered the war and passenger ships still travelled freely to Australia. Walter was very anxious about his mother. He wanted to see her for himself. He wanted to be assured that she was comfortable and well looked after by the relatives in America so he had paid for her to come to Australia for a visit. She was due to arrive in a few weeks' time and she would stay upstairs with Miriam while she was here. So when Miriam told him that he could not leave his marriage at this point of time, he knew she was right.

The imminent visit of Walter's mother caused Elizabeth's anguish to escalate. She was convinced that Walter's purpose in asking his mother to come to Australia was to get her to do something that he did not have the courage to do himself. Mother was being brought here to end the marriage. Elizabeth was convinced that this was true and she defended herself by abusing Walter with outbursts so venomous that Walter was shocked.

'My mother would never use language like that,' he declared.

'I'm not your mother,' said Elizabeth, 'I don't want to be like your mother.'

'That's the trouble,' said Walter. 'I married you because you reminded me of my mother and you're not like my mother at all!'

Actually, Mother saved, rather than destroyed, Elizabeth's marriage. Although it saddened her deeply to learn that Walter was unhappy she reinforced Miriam's view that a man does not leave a marriage once he has become the father of a child. He bowed to their opinion and he stayed with Elizabeth but from then on he behaved as if he were a bachelor. He did as he pleased. He offered no explanations for his comings and goings. Elizabeth continued to accuse him of sleeping with other women but he no longer denied her accusations and he no longer made any effort to hide what he was doing. If she wanted to stay married to him then she would have to accept that this was the way their marriage was going to be conducted.

Elizabeth hovered on the border of breakdown but some-how managed to keep herself within the boundaries of socially acceptable behaviour. Her hysterical outbursts were reserved for Walter and although he frequently reported them to his sister, she never actually witnessed them herself. Miriam went out with Walter whenever he asked her to do so because she knew he needed to confide in her but she stood firm in her belief that it was Walter who must adapt himself to the state of marriage. This conviction was reinforced by the fact that she was thirty-two years old herself and by the time Jacob got back from the war, assuming that he did survive that dan-gerous ordeal, she might well be too old to consider having children of her own. Jamie might be the only person in their branch of the family to carry on the Liebler name. He was a precious responsibility. His welfare must be paramount. So when Miriam was with Elizabeth, she behaved as if she knew nothing of their marital difficulties and Elizabeth, in turn, in face to face situations, always treated Miriam politely.

In fact, Elizabeth made herself adopt the persona of contented young wife and mother with everyone except Walter. If her family had lived in Sydney, rather than in Tasmania, she might not have been able to do so. She needed to prove, to her mother and to her sister, that her marriage was successful and she wrote them regular letters in which she lied about her relationship with Walter. The distance and the separation made the lies plausible, even to herself, and the very writing of the letters soothed her pain. Despite Walter's appalling behaviour, she continued to believe that she was in love with him and despite his obvious infidelities, she continued to see herself as the important woman in his life. She was, after all, his wife and the mother of his child. If she kept doing battle with him almost every time he entered the house then that was because of her blinding need to assert her rights and the rights of her child.

Jamie became a pawn in their conflicts. They vied with each other to claim his love. Walter entered the race with a handicap because he virtually ignored the baby until he was six months old, whereas Elizabeth had given him her love and attention from the moment he was born. Walter could not hope to penetrate the powerful bond that united mother and baby. Nor did he try. Indeed he admired Elizabeth's devotion to the child but he was determined to carve out a special place for himself in Jamie's heart and he proceeded to do that in a materialistic way. Firstly, Walter bought a pleasant, two-bedroomed cottage in one of the quieter streets in Chatswood. Jamie's bedroom was quite small but there was a large family room attached to the kitchen and this was to be Jamie's play area. There was a good sized, flat, safe backyard. Walter did not spend a great deal of time at home but when he did arrive he always bore gifts. Toys of all kinds. A variety of teddy bears, sets of coloured blocks, cars, trucks and fire engines.

'He doesn't need another car,' Elizabeth would complain. 'He's got too many already!'

'But look how happy it makes him. Look how he puts his hands out to take it. See! He's smiling. Listen to him chuckle. You can tell he likes it.'

'I keep telling you, Walter, that you're doing the wrong thing. You'll have to stop. His room's overflowing with toys. You don't know anything about Jamie's needs. What he needs is your time and attention. You don't give him much of that, do you! What makes you think that gifts can take the place of a father's love? I spend all my time with him. I give him love twenty-four hours a day and you waltz in here just when you feel like it and think you can win his love by bringing him toys!'

When Walter looked at Jamie, with his sturdy, compact body, his chubby hands, his full, rounded cheeks, he felt an awesome, silent love that he had no means of expressing. Walter had admired and respected his own father but physical contact had been minimal. It was a mother's role to fuss and fondle, to cuddle and console. A father kept his distance and, by doing so, taught his son how to become a man. Although he would have liked to sweep Jamie up into his arms, to hug him and kiss him and even to weep into the firm, fleshy folds of his neck, Walter could not do that. He was too afraid of being overwhelmed by his own emotions. But he could not have explained such a fear to Elizabeth. She might have laughed at him. So Walter continued to express his love for his son by providing him with material gifts and Jamie responded with a joyous willingness to receive anything that Walter was prepared to give him.

When Jamie grew into a tall, well built, little boy, Walter was quick to encourage an interest in sport. He bought the child a bicycle, cricket bats, footballs, soccer balls, tennis racquets and paid for swimming lessons. By the time Jamie started school, he knew that his father valued his sporting prowess above all else. He so longed for his father's love and approval that he did his best to excel in this area. It was not difficult. He loved to run, to swim, to play competitive games and, as he progressed through primary school, his passion for sport became so great that the success he achieved was not only for his father but also for himself.

There was, however, a driving need to please Walter because Jamie had come to blame himself, not only for his father's absences but also for the angry fights that seemed to occur whenever his father was in the house. Although these conflicts between his parents did not actually involve him, they often seemed to be about him and he could not help thinking that he was, in some way, the cause of their arguments. He thought that if he was very good, if he did what his father wanted him to do, then his father would want to spend more time at home. It was easy to please his mother. She always loved him and never criticised him but Walter was a different matter.

'Who did you fight with today?' his father would ask.

'I didn't fight with anyone,' Jamie would reply.

'How are you going to grow up to be a man if you don't fight with anyone?' his father wanted to know.

So Jamie would go off to school the next day and pick a fight with some boy, for no reason at all except to be able to go home that night and tell his father that he had fought one of his classmates and, moreover, won the fight. And then Walter wouldn't come home. He might be gone for a few days and

Jamie would have to pick a fight with another boy so that he'd be ready to tell his father what he wanted to hear the next time he did decide to come home.

Jamie was bewildered and confused by his father's absences. He knew that his father was a very busy man. He had three coffee lounges and they all stayed open late at night. Perhaps he was so tired after working all night that he slept at one of the coffee shops, rather than coming home. It was this staying away from home that made his mother so angry. And unhappy too. Sometimes she was so unhappy that she cried. He could not bear that. Seeing her tears. He wanted them to be happy together. He wanted that, more than anything in the world. He wanted to take his mother's hand and his father's hand and put those two hands together. He loved his mother and he loved his father and he could not understand why the two people he loved did not seem to love each other. Jamie's dream was to find a way to stop his parents from fighting with each other but, by the time he was ten years old, he had not been able to find a solution to the problem. And then, quite suddenly, without any warning, Jamie became ill.

The illness began on a Wednesday afternoon. Wednesday was sports day at school and Jamie had played a vigorous game of football. He was not yet old enough, big enough or strong enough to play in the school's 'A' team but he was a star of the Reserves and he'd helped to win a victory for his team by scoring two tries. He came home from school flushed but happy. Elizabeth looked at his sweat-streaked face, his glowing cheeks, his damp hair, his bright eyes and felt, as she always did, a surge of pride in her son.

'You look pleased with yourself,' she said.

'We won, Mum. Twenty to sixteen. I scored two tries and kicked one goal!'

'That's marvellous, Jamie. Daddy will be proud of you.'

As soon as the words came out of her mouth, Elizabeth hated herself for saying them. She wanted Jamie's achievement to be wonderful in itself, not related to how Walter would respond to it. Time and again she told herself that she must praise Jamie without reference to Walter's expectations yet somehow, like today, her own desire for Jamie to please his father made her say things that would have been better left unspoken. She tried to develop in Jamie interests and pursuits that Walter saw little value in. She praised the paintings and drawings that he did at school, encouraged his classroom efforts in composition and poetry writing, read him stories every night before he went to bed. Despite her efforts, Jamie saw such things as activities that girls, rather than boys, were interested in. A boy who spent too much time on painting and writing would be seen as a bit of a sissy. And that did not conform to Jamie's self image.

'It was a really difficult game,' said Jamie. 'I had to run so hard that my knees and ankles are aching.'

'Why don't you have a nice hot bath, Jamie. I'll put some Radox in it. Would you like that? Just lie in the tub and relax. That should take your aches and pains away.'

After he'd been in the bath for ten minutes, Jamie called out to Elizabeth.

'Mum, Mum! Will you come and dry me? I feel a bit dizzy.'

'The water must have been too hot,' said Elizabeth.

'I think I'll get into my pyjamas and lie down on the lounge in the playroom for a while,' said Jamie.

By 5.30 p.m. Jamie was crying out in pain. His knees and ankles hurt so badly that he couldn't get comfortable. He twisted and turned on the lounge. Elizabeth tried to cover him with a blanket but the weight of the blanket on his legs caused excruciating pain and he threw it off with a pitiful scream. She felt his forehead. It was burning hot.

She crushed two aspirins in a spoon, mixed them with honey and made him swallow them down. She got iceblocks from the freezer, wrapped them in a small towel, and held the cold compress to his forehead. She tried to hold his hand but he thrust her away as if her touch were fire. He said that his wrists were hurting. And his elbows as well. By 6 p.m. he felt a little cooler but the pain had not diminished. He thrashed about on the lounge. He could not bear to be still. She rang the local doctor and told him that he must come as soon as possible. She rang Walter and told him that he must come home at once. Jamie was desperately ill.

By the time the doctor arrived at 7 p.m. Jamie was delirious. His temperature was 103 degrees. The doctor thought that a flu virus was causing the high temperature and the aching limbs. Nothing could be done except to let it run its course. Elizabeth should keep giving him aspirin every four hours and, if his temperature remained high, she should put him in a bath of tepid water to cool his body down. Walter arrived home as the doctor was about to leave.

'You've got a very sick little boy there, Mr Liebler,' said the doctor. 'A bad dose of influenza. But I'm sure he'll be feeling a lot better by morning. I'll come and have a look at him early tomorrow, on my way to the surgery.'

Walter was still haunted by the nightmare of that night. He thought about it now, as he drove over to Zelda's apartment.

Whatever opinion he might have of Elizabeth as a wife, he had nothing but admiration for her as a mother. She had been magnificent. Calm. Strong. Controlled. He was the one who'd given way to panic. When he'd looked at Jamie writhing on the lounge he had turned away in horror. To his eternal shame, he had gone into their bedroom and closed the door to muffle the sounds of Jamie's high, shrill, incessant screams. He had sat down on the bed, unable to move. Perhaps it was hours later that Elizabeth had come into the room.

'You'll have to help me, Walter. I can't manage on my own.'

'What do I have to do?' whispered Walter.

'Go into the bathroom and run a cool bath. Fairly full. When you've done that come into the family room and help me carry him to the bath. His temperature is very high. I'll have to try to get it down.'

Walter could still feel the searing heat of Jamie's skin and the hot exhalation of his breath as he gathered the child up from the lounge to take him to the bathroom. Somehow he held onto Jamie while Elizabeth undressed him and together they slipped him into the bath. The cool water seemed to ease him momentarily and Elizabeth took a sponge and trickled water over Jamie's head and face, his shoulders and arms, while Walter supported him, as gently as possible, by holding him under the arms.

They'd had to repeat the procedure three times during the night. In the hours between the baths, Walter could not stay in the playroom. Elizabeth had guarded the child and tried to comfort him, while Walter sat in their bedroom with the door closed, waiting for Elizabeth to summon him. At 7 a.m. Elizabeth rang the doctor and told him that Jamie was worse. She wanted a paediatrician called in. She didn't care how much it cost. Jamie was in so much pain that he could not be moved. She said that the specialist would have to come to the house.

At 9 a.m. Dr Bradley arrived and recommended hospitalisation. His paediatric practice had access to a small, well equipped, private hospital in Greenwich. That was the place for Jamie to go. High temperatures in children of Jamie's age could be very dangerous. They could lead to convulsions. He should certainly be monitored for the next few days until they had determined the cause of his illness. He agreed with the local doctor that this was probably a severe case of influenza. There was every chance that Jamie would be back to normal within a week.

But Jamie hadn't recovered. The high temperatures had continued, day after day, and the pain in his arms and legs had not abated. At times his body shook with convulsive spasms and it seemed to Walter that no one knew how to help the child. He was angry with Elizabeth. He was angry with Dr Bradley. He was angry with himself because he could not bear to sit for hours beside Jamie's bed. He was even angry with Jamie for having contracted an illness that seemed to be so puzzling and so mysterious.

When Walter arrived at Zelda's place he expected to be comforted or, at the very least, to be distracted from his worry and concern over Jamie's health but Zelda was unusually quiet, almost sullen. Until a year ago, Walter would have described himself as a man who 'worked hard and played hard'. He was proud of his successful coffee lounges and he had made an enormous amount of money, much more than Elizabeth knew about. He was well on the way to becoming a millionaire and his aim was to put as much effort as possible into his business so that he could retire comfortably by the time he was fifty. Meeting Zelda, twelve months ago, had not changed his work habits but she had certainly changed his sexual behaviour. Gone was the need to sleep with as many women as possible. Zelda had so much to offer that she satisfied all his desires. She was twenty-nine years old, six years younger than Walter, but she'd certainly lived her life to the full. She'd travelled extensively and had enjoyed so many varied, sexual adventures that she was more than a match for Walter. He knew perfectly well that if he went off and slept with some other woman, then Zelda would have no qualms about evening the score. Satisfying Zelda's sexual appetite was a challenge and Walter did not want to risk failing her in this respect.

When Walter and Zelda began their affair, neither of them expected it to last. Walter was, after all, a married man and Zelda knew what to expect from married men. They were both surprised when they fell in love because they were both cynical about love. They were too pragmatic, too experienced to consider romantic love as a possibility. Walter found that he could tell Zelda anything and everything. He could confide in her in a way that was quite new to him. Intimacy. That's what he discovered with Zelda and once intimacy had been established neither he, nor Zelda, could contemplate a life without each other.

Zelda wanted him to leave Elizabeth and Jamie and to live with her. He aroused in her an urge to settle down and have children of her own. People did not have to remain in unhappy marriages. They could set themselves free and start again with a new love, a new life. She knew it would take time but she expected Walter to divorce Elizabeth and, eventually, to marry her.

Walter assured her that this was also what he wanted. He promised that he would make their dream come true. He had been on the brink of leaving Elizabeth when Jamie fell ill and now Jamie's condition had set him back. He could not take the final step of moving out while Jamie's health was so precarious. His procrastination had upset Zelda. That's why she was sulking.

'Don't be so cranky with me, Zelda. I can't help it. I'm sick with worry about my son.'

'It's not that.'

'What is it then? What's the matter?'

'I wanted today to be a day of celebration,' said Zelda, 'and instead it's full of gloom and sadness.'

'Celebration?'

'I've had a pregnancy test, Walter. It was positive. We're going to have a baby.'

Walter knelt down in front of Zelda, put his head in her lap and, quite unexpectedly, broke into deep, harsh sobs. He wept uncontrollably. Zelda stroked his head and soothed him until the weeping came to an end. He could not have explained his outburst. Joy and sorrow were so intermingled that he could not separate his emotions. His fear for Jamie and his longing for the birth of this new child both made their claims on him and he felt as if his heart was being torn apart.

Walter got his way. Jamie was moved to the Children's Hospital. The doctors there tried penicillin in the hope that his condition had been caused by an infection.

'If you'd listened to me, Elizabeth, Jamie would have come here in the first place. If he'd been given penicillin straight away he'd be cured by now,' said Walter.

'You don't know what you're talking about, Walter. And you can stop blaming me. It's not my fault. You know I've done everything possible to help Jamie. If you want to start blaming someone, have a good look at yourself. How much time have you devoted to our son over the last few weeks?'

After five days there was no change. Jamie's temperature remained high. The joints remained painful. Warm compresses and pain-killers brought some relief. They knocked him out with sleeping pills every night to allow him some respite from the pain. The doctors came to the conclusion that there was only one explanation for Jamie's condition. He was suffering from Still's disease, juvenile rheumatoid arthritis.

Definition: Rheumatoid arthritis is a systemic disease of unknown origin in which symptoms and inflammatory change predominate in articular and related structures. Tends to be chronic and result in characteristic deformities. There is a familial tendency in rheumatoid arthritis.

Pathology: Lesions result in thickening of synovial membrane, destruction of cartilage and bone. A layer of granulation tissue, called pannus, begins to invade and destroy cartilage, presumably interfering with its proper nutrition. Ossification takes place in the adhesion.

Etiology: Cause remains unknown. Some say it is linked with infection but this is not proved. Some say it is due to some derangement of the immunologic mechanism of a person but this is not proved.

Clinical Features: In some patients acute and fulminating, with high fever, intense joint inflammation, rapid evolution of deformities. Knees, hands and feet usually sites of initial attack. Once affected, joint tends to remain inflamed for weeks, months or years. Deformities usually occur at wrists, elbows, knees.

The skin, especially over the extremities, is cool, pale and clammy. Over the fingers the skin appears taut and shiny. Muscle aching, tenderness, stiffness occur – prominent throughout the disease. Muscular atrophy and weakness may be striking. High incidence of cardiac lesions.

Management: Efforts are directed toward (1) assuring proper amounts of rest and exercise (2) the relief of pain (3) combating the rheumatoid process (4) preventing deformities (5) correcting deformities which have developed (6) controlling complications (7) maintaining nutrition and (8) rehabilitating the patient.

Relief of pain: Pain relief is important in itself and must be achieved before active physical therapy can be undertaken. Application of heat to alleviate pain. Addictive drugs to be avoided. Since pain is largely the result of inflammation, drugs chosen should be anti-inflammatory as well as analgesic. Salicylates, phenylbutazone (butazolodin and andrenocortical steroids). Cortisone, prednisone – maintenance doses.

Still's disease: Juvenile rheumatoid arthritis begins in children before puberty and comprises 4% of all cases of rheumatoid arthritis. Systemic symptoms and signs are more severe in the juvenile than in the adult form. Fever often spikes daily at 105 degrees and may continue for months. Growth and development may be impaired. Satisfactory functional recovery occurs in three quarters of all patients.

Jamie's case fell into the category of the one quarter of patients who do not recover. He was to remain in hospital for two years.

CHAPTER 2

Walter blamed Elizabeth for Jamie's disease. There was no history of rheumatoid arthritis in his family. Nothing of the kind. The doctors had asked him and he'd been able to assure them that, as far as he knew, none of his relatives had ever had anything like this. But could Elizabeth give the same assurances? No, she could not. She'd had osteomyelitis, hadn't she? She'd been left with abnormal ankle joints. It was her genes that had passed on to Jamie some tendency, some predisposition, some vulnerability to the ravages of this terrible illness. Walter was sure of that. There was nothing wrong with the Liebler genes.

And now his beautiful, perfect boy would be crippled and deformed. After several months of conservative treatment, Jamie had been given a drug called A.C.T.H. The doctors hadn't wanted to use it but the child did not respond to anything else. They'd warned Walter and Elizabeth that prolonged use of this cortisone treatment would stunt Jamie's growth. Of course that side effect of the drug would not be a problem for a few years because Jamie was quite tall for a ten-year-old. Slight deformities were already discernible in his elbows, wrists and knees. They were certainly obvious to Walter. But at least the A.C.T.H. had worked. At last the high temperatures had ceased, the pain had eased a little and it was possible to begin slow, gentle rehabilitation of the joints and muscles. Jamie was so weak and exhausted by the illness that Walter did not believe he would ever achieve a meaningful recovery. When he looked at his son, Walter felt so bereft of hope that he found himself wishing the boy would die.

Elizabeth did not share Walter's pessimism. She sat by Jamie's bed, day after day. She gave him her love, her devotion, her energy and she tried to instil in him her great desire for him to get well. She ceased to take any notice of Walter's comings and goings. Her focus on Jamie was intense and absolute.

Zelda's pregnancy was well advanced by the time Walter found the courage to talk to Elizabeth about the future. He chose to speak to her one night as he was driving her home from the hospital.

'Elizabeth,' he said, 'I want a divorce.'

'How can you bring up a subject like that when Jamie is so ill,' said Elizabeth.

'I've met someone else. A woman I really love. She's going to have my child. I'm going to leave you and live with her. I want a divorce.'

'Don't be ridiculous, Walter. You have a wife. You have a child. Jamie is the only person you should be thinking of right now.'

'Elizabeth, I can't go on being married to you. I'll always look after you financially. You and Jamie will have everything you need.' And although Walter came into the house, packed all his clothes into suitcases and drove away, Elizabeth did not really believe that he had left her. How could he abandon her when Jamie's illness was so obviously going to be prolonged, difficult and demanding? The very idea of Walter leaving them at such a time was incomprehensible. She had to accept that he was serious, however, when letters started arriving from his lawyer, setting out financial arrangements and suggesting that Elizabeth seek the services of a divorce lawyer. She was informed that she could sue for divorce on the grounds of Walter's adultery with Zelda. This would be the quickest and easiest way to end the marriage. Elizabeth decided to ignore the lawyer's letters.

A week later, Walter telephoned Elizabeth early in the morning, before she'd left for the hospital, because he was reluctant to discuss the matter with her in front of Jamie.

'Are you going to agree to a divorce, Elizabeth?'

'You're my husband, Walter. As far as I'm concerned you'll always be my husband,' Elizabeth replied.

'But Zelda's baby is due very soon.'

'That's your problem, Walter, not mine.'

'Have you told Jamie that I've left you?' Walter wanted to know.

'Certainly not,' replied Elizabeth. And she hung up the phone.

So Walter was left with the task of explaining to Jamie that he loved another woman and that he was going to be the father of another child. He did it rather clumsily with the result that he had to flee from the hospital room when Jamie reacted to the unpleasant news by screaming hysterically, 'No! No! You can't do that! You can't! You can't!' Walter tried to placate Jamie by visiting more frequently and by showering him with gifts but Jamie became sullen and uncooperative. The anger he felt towards his father turned into anger against himself. He looked at his weak and feeble body with loathing and disgust. Would he ever be strong enough to run again? To swim? To play football? And if he couldn't do those things then how was he ever going to be able to win back his father's love? He became depressed and despondent but the doctors, nurses and physiotherapists ignored his occasional outbursts of aggressive behaviour and continued to offer encouragement and support. And then, of course, there was his mother, whose love and patience were boundless. Gradually Jamie recovered sufficient strength and mobility to be able to leave hospital, just after his twelfth birthday.

'I'm not going to call you "Jamie" any more,' said Elizabeth. 'You're going to be the man in our house and you must have your proper, grown-up name. I'm going to call you "James" from now on.'

Jamie was fearful and anxious about returning to school. His rehabilitation had included tutoring for several hours each day and he hoped that he would be able to keep up with the schoolwork. His real anguish lay in wondering how to behave in the playground. Would the boys in his class accept him if he could no longer participate in the games that boys traditionally played? Although he'd been away from school for two years, they must remember what he had been like. What would they think of him now? He could walk normally and the deformities in his joints were obvious only if you looked at them very closely. He was now short for his age, rather than tall, but not so short that anyone would remark on it. He could pass for almost normal but participation in sport was, for the time being, both forbidden and impossible. He would have to be an observer, unable to join the other boys in vigorous, physical play. And the illness had focussed his attention on his own body in a way that was both obsessive and unhealthy. Every movement he made was a conscious movement; every step that he took was a deliberate step and pain was a constant companion.

At first everyone was kind to him. His teachers and his fellow students had been informed about his illness and the nature of his physical limitations. Initially they regarded him as an interesting curiosity. Within a few weeks, however, they were treating him the way people always behave towards those amongst them who are less than perfect. They simply ignored him. Social isolation was painful but the physical effort of getting through a school day was so exhausting that Jamie had to spend recess and lunchtime sitting on a bench in the playground, head resting against the wall, eyes closed, trying to recover sufficient energy to survive the next few hours. He would return home to his mother, pale and tearful.

'I'm so proud of you, James,' she would say. 'I can't tell you how much I admire the effort you're making. It will get easier, you know. You'll become stronger and stronger. And next year, you'll be going to high school. High school is much more interesting than primary school. You can learn languages and science and art. You'll be much happier when you go to high school.'

'I'm so tired,' he would say.

'I know,' Elizabeth would reply. And then a gaping silence would open up between them and they each filled that silence with the unspoken terror that Jamie's situation might not improve, that he might never be strong enough to lead a normal life, that his physical abnormalities might become more pronounced, that he might continue to be isolated and rejected by his peers.

He was never able to attend school for a full week. Elizabeth noted, but did not comment on the fact that his pain always seemed too great to go to school on Wednesdays. She could not blame him for lacking the courage to deal with sports days. She had to be Jamie's friend and companion, his constant and never failing source of support. She took him to museums and art galleries, to concerts, theatres and cinemas. Sometimes he would refuse to go with her.

'I'm sick of going out with you! Sick to death of always being with my mother. Other boys have friends to go out with.

They go to watch football and cricket. I'm sick of seeing stupid plays in stupid theatres!'

Elizabeth understood these outbursts but she could not help being hurt by them. Everything she did was directed towards making Jamie's life more bearable. It was painful to be reminded that she could neither fulfil his needs nor compensate him for his suffering. She treated him as an adult and was distressed when he behaved like a child. She often wept in bed at night, tears of frustration and anguish. Jamie could hear her crying and her sadness made him uneasy. He blamed himself for her sorrow and told himself that he mustn't get angry with her. She was, after all, his only friend and she loved him always, no matter what he did.

That wasn't true of his father. Jamie could tell that his physical pain and slowness were a constant source of irritation to his father. Every Sunday was spent with Walter and his new family. Jamie approached these visits with mixed feelings. He longed for his father's love and attention and it was quite clear to Jamie that Walter saw him as someone towards whom he owed a very special duty. Tears would well up in his father's eyes and Jamie would have to look away in embarrassment. He didn't want to be pitied. He wanted to be loved.

And love was what he witnessed in his father's new family. He wanted to hate Zelda but she was so nice to him that he could not help liking her. He resented the fact that his father had another child but Katie was fourteen months old before he met her. She had just taken her first steps and she held her arms out to him, laughing and gurgling, and then falling down flat on her bottom. She won his heart in an instant. His father didn't argue with Zelda. There were none of the parental fights and confrontations that had been the norm when his mother and father were living together. Instead they spoke lovingly to each other, touched each other on passing, deferred to each other's opinions. And he wanted to be jealous about the new house, which was far more splendid than the one he shared with his mother, but his father had installed a heated swimming pool and made Jamie feel that he had done this purely for his son's benefit. Jamie could swim there on Sundays and should feel free to come any time he pleased, every day after school if he wanted to. Walter felt sure that swimming would help Jamie to grow stronger. Aunty Miriam and Uncle Jacob were always there for Sunday lunch and they were such good fun that he enjoyed being with them. The food was plentiful and delicious. It seemed to Jamie that his father's new life was full of laughter and joy. He wished he could take hold of that happiness and keep it inside himself forever.

When his father dropped him home, late on a Sunday afternoon, Jamie often felt irritable and angry. His mother would plague him with questions. 'What did you do? What did you eat? Who was there? What was that woman wearing? Is she beautiful? What about the baby? Who does the baby look like? Tell me about the house. What colour is the carpet? What sort of furniture do they have?' One Sunday, he felt he couldn't put up with his mother's questions any longer.

'Leave me alone. I don't want to talk about it,' said Jamie.

'You don't have to go there, James. You can refuse. If you come back upset every Sunday then I can only assume that going to your father's place is not good for you.'

'I said, "Leave me alone!" If you want to know what his house is like and what his wife is like and what his baby is like then go there and have a look for yourself!'

'You know I can't do that,' said Elizabeth.

'Well, stop asking me. I'm not going to tell you. And if you want to know the truth, I like going there. It's not going to Dad's that upsets me. It's all your stupid questions.' And Jamie went into his room, slammed the door and lay down on his bed, his heart pounding, his eyes brimming with tears. He knew exactly what expression his mother would have on her face at this very moment. It would be the hurt, disappointed look that crept into her eyes and into the corners of her mouth whenever he was angry with her. He didn't want to hurt her but he couldn't help it. Coming back home, after a day at his father's, made his mother and the house they lived in seem drab and ordinary. Everything here was dull and grey and serious, whereas his father's house, and the people in it, were bathed in a golden, airy, magical light that buoyed his spirits. He longed for the impossible, for his father to love his mother and himself instead of loving Zelda and baby Katie, for Zelda and her child to disappear. He wanted to take their place and live with his father and mother in the golden harmony of that splendid new house.

And then he looked down at his knobbly knees, at the white skin stretched taut across his fingers, at the protruding bones of his wrists and elbows. He hated what he saw. A boy like him had no place in a golden world. He thought about his mother and himself and the fact that his father had left them for a new life and he said to himself, 'Our hearts died when you left.' Although it was a very difficult thing for him to do, he got up and went out to his mother. He put his arms around her.

'I'm sorry, Mum,' he said, and they both wept until Elizabeth managed to pull herself together. She took out her handkerchief and wiped away their tears.

'Why don't we go to that nice Italian place at Crows Nest for dinner? You love their pizza, don't you?'

'I sure do,' said Jamie. 'And can I stay up tonight and watch a film on T.V.?'

'It's school tomorrow,' said Elizabeth.

'Please, Mum, please. I promise to be well enough to go to school.'

'Alright then. Just as a special treat.'

Elizabeth brushed her hair, arranged it into a neat bun, put on some lipstick and went out to the car with Jamie. Thank goodness they had a car. Her decision to comply with Walter's wishes and sue for divorce so that he could marry Zelda had resulted in great benefit to herself and Jamie. Walter had paid off the mortgage and transferred the house to her name, bought her this brand new little car and provided her with a generous weekly allowance that more than met their needs. If she wanted money for anything else she only had to ask. Each Sunday morning, when he came to pick up Jamie, he would spend half an hour sitting with her in the lounge room. They would have a cup of tea together and they were able to engage in perfectly civil, friendly, impersonal conversations.

The truth of the matter was that Jamie's illness had changed Elizabeth forever. His welfare was all she cared about. She saw Walter as a wayward man who had somehow been trapped by another woman. In a small place, in her own heart, she continued to believe that she was his lawful wife and Jamie his lawful son. These other people, Zelda and the new child, were somehow secondary, unimportant upstarts. One day Walter would see the error of his ways and return to her and Jamie, his rightful family. She could not, however, help but be curious about Zelda and the child. It was obviously Walter's intention to keep them away from her. She had not even seen photographs of them. And she did not know that Walter's new house was palatial compared to her own because both Walter and Jamie had kept that knowledge from her. Although she was curious she would have found it personally demeaning to spy on them. The one thing she was determined on, however, was that neither she, nor Jamie, would suffer financially because of Walter's transgressions. As long as he fulfilled these material obligations she would, for the moment, try to overcome her curiosity about his new life. She was angry with herself tonight. She must stop questioning Jamie about his father's life.

By the time Jamie began high school, at the age of thirteen, it was quite clear that he suffered a deformity. The prolonged use of A.C.T.H. had caused osteoporosis of the spine and pelvis with the result that his hips looked abnormally small and his legs abnormally short when compared with the size of his head and torso. Regular swimming in his father's pool had developed his chest and shoulder muscles and this further accentuated the top-heavy look of his body. He was not so short that he would be regarded as a midget or a dwarf but if you looked at him, and people certainly did look, you knew that there was something wrong.

That was the hardest part for Jamie. Being stared at. Then having the person who was staring at you look away and pretend you didn't exist. Ignore you completely. Why did people do that? What were they afraid of? He was just the same as they were underneath. They were all scared about starting high school. Jamie looked around at the hundred or so boys and girls assembled together on their first day of their first year at high school and he prayed that he might find some way of being accepted by them.

The first few days were agonising. He spoke to no one. No one spoke to him. On the fourth day he was sitting on a bench in the playground, eating his lunch, when a girl from his class came over and stood in front of him.

'Can I sit down and have lunch with you? I'm a bit sick of being on my own,' she said.

'You're in my class, aren't you,' said Jamie.

'Yes, I thought you mightn't have noticed me. I always try to get into the classroom quickly so I can sit right up the back. And you seem to have a bit of trouble getting up the stairs so you're always a few minutes late. I thought maybe you hadn't realised we're in the same class.'

'Why do you always sit up the back?'

'Because I'm so tall. If I sat in front of anyone they'd never be able to see the teacher,' she laughed. And she was tall. So tall that he couldn't have helped noticing her. Over a foot taller than anyone else in the class. And thin. Her chest was flat and her hips were narrow as if all the growth hormones in her body had directed their attention towards increasing her height. 'A beanpole, that's what I am.' And she laughed again. 'My name's Judy, by the way, and I know yours. You're James.'

'I suppose everyone notices me,' said James.

'Well, they stare at me too,' said Judy.

'Only you can laugh about it.'

'My mum told me she was just like me when she was my age. People develop at different rates, that's all. In a few years' time I won't be so tall and thin that everyone thinks I'm a freak. I'll be tall and beautiful, my mum says, and by then the other girls will have caught up a bit. You have to keep your sense of humour. That's the only way. What's wrong with you anyway?'

'I've got rheumatoid arthritis,' said Jamie. 'I got it when I was ten.'

'Is that bad?'

'It could be. I'm not going to grow up to be tall and beautiful,' said Jamie. Judy laughed when he said that and he realised he'd made a joke at his own expense.

'That's the way,' she said. 'Have a laugh at yourself. People don't stare at you to be cruel, you know. They just don't know how to deal with someone who's different from themselves.' Then the bell rang to mark the end of lunchtime. Judy got up quickly. 'You take your time, James. I'm going to dash in and get that seat I like in the back row. I'll keep you a place next to me. Alright?'

It was more than alright. It was great. It was wonderful. It was fantastic. As James laboured up the stairs to his classroom his heart sang and his spirits soared. At last he had a friend.

Sitting next to Judy made all the difference in the world. Between classes they talked and laughed and joked. Their enjoyment in each other's company was so obvious that other students were drawn to them and tentatively joined in their conversations. Soon camaraderie developed in the classroom and Jamie found that he was neither excluded nor isolated. The playground, however, was a different matter. He was aware of how incongruous he and Judy appeared to be to others. He knew that their friendship was viewed as a union of misfits and this was borne out by the fact that the goodwill exhibited in the classroom was not extended to social contact in the playground. Jamie and Judy spent recesses and lunchtimes alone together.

One friend, however, was better than no friends and Judy was a very loyal friend indeed. There were many days when

Jamie was in too much pain to go to school and on those days she would always ring to find out how he was, to offer support, to say she hoped he'd be back at school tomorrow. They visited each other's houses and often went to the movies together on Saturday afternoons. Judy played the piano and she persuaded Jamie to take an interest in the music club at school. He decided to learn the guitar. His father agreed to buy him an instrument and pay for private lessons when he showed some musical aptitude. He and Judy began playing in the school band and this helped to win him partial acceptance. Judy remained his best friend but other associations were formed. By the time Jamie was fifteen he had begun to hope that his physical disadvantages were not so great that they would prevent him from leading a satisfactory social life.

Jamie was getting taller. He had now reached a height of 5'2" but he was not expected to grow any more than this. The thing that really bothered him was his failure to develop sexually. His doctors at the Children's Hospital had always been honest with him. They monitored his progress at regular check-ups and kept assuring him that sexual development would occur, although the drugs used to control his arthritis had, inevitably, caused delay. This did not comfort him. He looked with envy at the downy hair on the upper lips and cheeks of his classmates.

And he was embarrassed by the way Walter dealt with the problem. He would charge into the bedroom where Jamie changed after his Sunday swim in the pool, on some barely legitimate pretext, and take a surreptitious look at Jamie's genitals. Had they grown in size in the last week? Was there any hair under the boy's arms? Any sign at all that his son was going to develop into a normal man? Jamie wanted to protest. He longed to shout at his father, 'Get out of here! Stop staring at me!' but he was so paralysed by humiliation that he was unable to utter a word. It was always like that. He could never tell his father what he really felt. He knew that Walter cared about him. He knew that his illness was the constant source of his father's worry and concern. But they couldn't talk about such things. They could only skirt around the subject, never face it.

There was a great deal of discussion about the future. Walter assured Jamie that each month he put any extra money he had into buying stocks and shares in Jamie's name so that his financial future would be secure, if anything happened to prevent him from earning an income of his own. But he hoped that wouldn't occur. When Jamie left school, Walter would take him into the business. He'd start Jamie at the bottom and gradually teach him all he needed to know about managing coffee lounges. They'd work together. Father and son.

Jamie also felt a little easier about his own physical shortcomings because baby Katie had proved to have an imperfection of her own. Walter's house was in Cremorne Point, overlooking the harbour and sailing boats were clearly visible through his lounge room window. One day, when Katie was two years old, Jamie had held her up to watch a sailing race taking place in the water below the house.

'No boats,' said Katie.

'What do you mean, Katie? Look, there are lots of boats down there racing against each other. Look at that! They're turning and putting up their spinnakers. There's a black and gold one and that red one over there. Aren't they beautiful?'

'No boats,' Katie insisted.

A visit to an eye specialist revealed that Katie suffered from such severe myopia that it would be necessary for her to wear spectacles at all times. Walter was distraught.

'How can she be so short sighted? She's only two years old. Those glasses look so ugly! Take them off, Zelda, when she's inside the house. She doesn't need to wear them all day long!'

'But she does, Walter. She's almost blind without them,' said Zelda.

'Her eyes will get weaker if she wears them all the time,' said Walter. 'Eye exercises. That's what she needs. Strengthen those eye muscles. Then her sight will improve.' And Katie responded by tearing off her glasses whenever her father was around, so that he wouldn't be angry, and then crying in frustration because she couldn't see without them. Jamie watched the development of this conflict with a mixture of relief and apprehension. He identified with Katie's anxiety and her desire to please her father. His bond with her intensified because now they both fell short of Walter's expectations. And yet there was an element of perverse satisfaction, an almost wicked pleasure in knowing that the perfect child of Walter's perfect second marriage was not so perfect after all.

Somewhere in the middle of his fifteenth year, development occurred and it happened so swiftly that, to Jamie, it seemed nothing short of a miracle. Dark hair sprouted from his armpits and groin, a beard seemed to appear overnight, his voice deepened, his testicles became heavy and comfortably filled the sacks beneath his rapidly thickening and growing penis. Sperm came unbidden in the darkness of a joyous, sensual dream and soiled his pyjama pants. Riotous, sexual yearnings raced through his body and so wondrous was the feel of his own hard penis in his eager, trembling hand that he brought himself to thrilling orgasm every night before he went to sleep.

The change was obvious to everyone and Walter was unable to conceal his delight. He hugged Jamie to his chest, his voice choked with tears, as he whispered, 'At last you are a man.' Jamie held back, momentarily embarrassed, and then found himself surrendering to Walter's display of emotion. He clung to his father and hugged him unreservedly. When they drew apart, Jamie discovered that his own cheeks were wet with tears.

Jamie did not discuss his sexual feelings with anyone but he could examine the subject of love with his friend, Judy. 'Do you think any girl will ever love me?' he asked her, during one of their deep and meaningful conversations about life.

'What about me? I haven't improved over the last few years, have I! I still look like a freak. My chest is almost as flat as a pancake and I still tower over everyone else. No boy will ever love me.'

'People should love you for what you are inside. Not for what you look like,' said Jamie.

'I know, but it doesn't work like that. It's appearance that matters. There's no getting away from it. It's the good-looking kids at school who have relationships. People like us just get left out. It's so depressing,' said Judy.

'I think we're more mature than the others,' said Jamie. 'We realise what's really important about a person and they haven't learned that yet.' But Jamie knew that Judy was right. Although there were several girls at school whom he felt attracted to he was sure they would all refuse him if he asked them to go out with him. Even the ordinary, unattractive girls would reject him. So he imagined what it would be like to make love to them. He conjured up their faces, their breasts, their thighs and made them into objects of his fantasy life without any hope or expectation that he would ever have the opportunity to turn fantasy into reality.

On his sixteenth birthday, however, his father offered him that opportunity. Walter suggested to Jamie that a visit to a brothel might be a very appropriate sixteenth birthday present for a father to give to his son. Jamie was shocked and embarrassed when Walter made this proposition. He had to look away and stare out of the car window while Walter elaborated on the subject.

'Sex is natural, Jamie. It's part of life. An important part of life. A boy needs to know what it's like to make love to a woman and the sooner he learns the better. I had to wait until I was eighteen and I know how awful that was. I was dying to know what it would be like. And the first woman I ever slept with was six years older than me. She knew what to do. It's much better to do it the first time with a woman who's experienced. That's why I thought I'd take you to an expert.'

'I don't know, Dad. I always thought I'd wait until I really loved someone,' said Jamie.

'Love, Jamie? Love? There's love and there's sex and what a boy your age needs is sex, sex and more sex.'

'I'll think about it, Dad.'

'If you wait until you meet some girl you love, she'll be a virgin and you'll be a virgin and you'll both be fumbling around not knowing what to do. Believe me, it's better for a man to be experienced. Besides, I've arranged it all. Just be ready next Saturday afternoon at three o'clock.'

What Walter did not reveal to Jamie was his real motivation. He saw his boy as crippled and deformed and he did not believe that any woman would ever willingly make love to him. He hoped that, by introducing him to the world in which sex was a commodity, he could show Jamie that this was an acceptable way to achieve sexual gratification. There was no doubt in Walter's mind that Jamie would always have to purchase and pay for a woman's sexual favours.

There were six days to wait until next Saturday afternoon and those days were filled with anguish. Several times Jamie went to the phone to ring his father, to tell him to cancel the arrangements but somehow he couldn't dial the number. He didn't want to disappoint his father and yet he knew that it would be impossible for him to do what his father expected him to do. Much as he wanted to know what it would be like to put his penis inside a woman's vagina, he could not expose himself to some woman he did not know, some woman who had been paid to service him in this way. He believed in love. He longed for love and, in the very core of his being, he was sure that some day, some woman would look beyond his body and see into his soul and find that his soul was beautiful. And this woman who recognised his inner beauty would regard his physical shortcomings as unfortunate but irrelevant. The ability of two souls to know and understand each other would transcend the physical. He would love that woman and she would love him and then he would be ready to learn the meaning of sexual union. He could not have said all this to his father. Walter was too powerful, too sure of himself, too certain that he knew what was best for Jamie. So throughout the six days, the proposed visit to the prostitute dominated Jamie's mind and he tried to think of some way of getting around the situation.

Walter had not approached this matter lightly. He had given consideration to Jamie's youth, his vulnerability and the anxiety that might accompany losing his virginity in this way. He had, in fact, interviewed several women in different suburban brothels before making his selection. As he drove Jamie to the woman he had chosen, on that Saturday afternoon, he tried to reassure the boy, tried to make him feel more comfortable about the whole thing by telling him what trouble he'd taken to find a woman who would be sympathetic to the fact that Jamie suffered from an illness that had left him a bit disabled, a bit different from normal men.

'You mean that you actually told her there's something wrong with me?' Jamie was appalled.

'Well, yes,' said Walter. 'I thought it was better to be honest.'

Walter pulled up outside a perfectly ordinary looking Darlinghurst terrace house. 'I'll come up with you and introduce you to Helen. And then I'll wait out here in the car. Take your time. I've brought the newspaper to read.'

Jamie was so humiliated that he wished the ground would split open and swallow him up. He wanted to be anywhere in the world except here. He allowed himself to be ushered out of the car but the only way he could deal with his present circumstances was by detaching himself from his body. He stepped outside of himself and, as if from a distance, he watched himself and his father as they made their way up the steps. Walter knocked on the door. Jamie's defence of depersonalisation was working so well that he felt numb, entirely devoid of feeling.

A woman opened the door. She wore jeans and a white T-shirt and she looked so ordinary that Jamie's first thought was that she couldn't possibly be a prostitute. She was about thirty years old.

'Hello, Jamie, come in. I'm Helen,' she said and she took Jamie's hand and drew him inside while, with the other hand, she firmly closed the front door, leaving Walter standing on the doorstep. She took Jamie into a large room with an ordinary looking double bed in the left-hand corner. On the right-hand side of the room there were two comfortable looking small armchairs with a coffee table in front of them.

'Let's sit here and have a bit of a chat,' she said. She sat down in one of the armchairs, leaned back, crossed her legs and lit a cigarette. She gestured towards the other chair and Jamie, somewhat relieved to find that Helen was not at all intimidating, sat down awkwardly on the edge of his armchair.

'Look, this is all my Dad's idea. I don't even want to be here,' said Jamie.

'Well, we don't have to do anything that you don't want to do,' said Helen. 'It's up to you.'

'Could we just talk, then, for as long as it would have taken and then I could go back out and pretend I'd done it.'

'We could do that. No problem. All the same, it was nice of your Dad to arrange for you to come here. There aren't many dads who'd do something like this for their kid. And it's not so scary, really, you know. It just seems sort of frightening because you've never done it before.'

'But he told you I'm crippled! I know he did,' said Jamie.

'You don't look too crippled to me. You don't look as if there's much wrong with you at all,' said Helen.

'Don't I? Don't I really?' said Jamie.

'I tell you what. If you want to just talk, we'll just talk but if you like I'll turn around and you can take off your clothes and hop into bed. I'll come in with you. It's rather cosy, you know, chatting in bed.'

'I'm not sure,' said Jamie.

'If you like,' said Helen, 'I'll go out of the room for a few minutes while you decide whether you want to get into bed or not. O.K.?'

'O.K.' said Jamie.

'And whatever you decide, that's alright with me, O.K.?'

'O.K.' said Jamie.

When Helen left the room, Jamie really didn't know what he was going to do. He continued to sit on the edge of his chair for a moment or two and then he suddenly got up, took off his shoes and socks, his trousers and shirt and jumped into bed, still wearing his underpants for protection. When Helen returned she undressed in a swift, matter of fact way and got into bed beside him.

'Have you got a boyfriend?' Jamie asked.

'Actually, I'm married. I've got two little kiddies,' Helen replied. 'They're two and four. A bit of a handful. I just work weekends. To earn a bit of extra money. My husband minds the kids while I'm here.'

'Doesn't he mind? About your working here, I mean,' Jamie asked.

'Not really. You see I met him through my work. He was twenty-eight years old and he'd never made love to a woman. Can you believe that? He was so shy. You've no idea. And I fell in love with him. There and then. You see, Jamie, I like to think I'm helping people, people like my husband, people like you.'

Jamie had no idea whether Helen was telling him the truth or not but he was ready to believe anything she said to him. She certainly had the knack of making him feel that she was quite happy to be sharing a bed with him. She did not kiss him on the lips but smiled at him, kissed the tip of his nose and his forehead in a friendly way and then put her arm around him.

'I don't think we need these, do we? ' she said, as she deftly removed his underpants. She lay on her side and drew Jamie's body close in towards her. When he felt her soft, heavy breasts against his chest and her warm belly pressed against him, he responded with an immediate erection. They remained on their sides while she expertly guided his penis into her vagina. She took hold of his buttocks and held him firmly while his penis thrust inside her for only a few moments before ejaculation.

'There now,' said Helen, 'that wasn't too bad, was it?'

'It was great,' said Jamie.

She gave him a brief hug, got out of bed and put on her clothes. 'I'll wait outside while you're getting dressed, Jamie. Just come out when you're ready.'

When Jamie left the house and walked down the steps to the car, he had a small, embarrassed smile on his face.

'Well?' said Walter, as he let Jamie into the car.

'I did it!' said Jamie, and his face broke into a huge grin.

'Good boy!' said Walter. And they grinned and laughed all the way home. Jamie thought that his father was right. There was sex and there was love and even without love, sex was pretty good. In fact, it was terrific. Jamie hoped, however, that the next time he had sex, love would also be involved. He did not, of course, tell Walter that. His father might not have understood.

Although Jamie completed the five years of high school he did not enjoy schoolwork and he did not do well academically. There were no more acute arthritic attacks and no more trips to hospital but painful joints meant frequent absences and the effort of catching up on missed work became too exhausting to contemplate. Elizabeth had hoped that Jamie might develop a particular love for a particular subject, something that would capture his imagination, sweep him away to a life of passionate interest and involvement. But that did not happen. And his initial aptitude for the guitar did not develop beyond the mediocre. For a while he tried to compose songs of his own but his music was derivative, his lyrics mundane and often, of course, his fingers were too sore and swollen to pluck the guitar strings.

Jamie was obsessed with his physical shortcomings and he could not look beyond them. He wanted the impossible. He wanted to run and jump and play football but he would never be able to do those things. He wanted to be tall, strong and handsome but he was short, weak and misshapen. His own body disgusted him and if he loathed himself then he could not expect anyone else to approach him with anything less than aversion. He was often depressed. He was often angry. Elizabeth bore the brunt of his anger because she understood his despair. His anger took the form of dark-humoured self-mockery and he frequently expressed his frustration by directing his anger towards God, the universe and the general unfairness of existence. Why him? Why had he (rather than someone else) been condemned to live a life of pain in a monstrous body? He tortured himself by the constant asking of haunting, unanswerable questions. He could see no meaning in his life. There was no clear direction to follow. So when he left school he agreed to go and work with his father because he had to do something. Normality was the only thing he craved and he could never have that. When he contemplated the millions of years of dark emptiness that had existed before he was born then he wanted to return to that void of oblivion. He did not desire death. Having been born, he clung onto life but he wished, quite frankly, that his birth had never taken place.

Working for his father had moments of satisfaction although, on the whole, he found his father difficult and demanding. Jamie was not terribly interested in the business and therefore did not learn with the speed or the alacrity that Walter expected of him. He liked the atmosphere of the coffee lounges. He liked talking to the waitresses. He liked the kudos that went along with being the boss's son. He liked the busy, bustling hours when the coffee lounges were full of talk and smoke. He began to smoke himself and the job he most preferred was sitting at the cash register, taking in the money, smoking cigarettes and simply observing people come and go.

The very best thing about working for his father was the M.G. sports car that had been bought for him so that he could drive himself to and from work and from one coffee lounge to another. He dashed around the city, taking corners at dangerous speeds and spent the weekends tearing up and down country highways.

The car was his comfort and his consolation. It was also the means by which he was able to hold onto and maintain a fragile network of friends. Girls who would never otherwise have agreed to go out with him now sought his company because of the car. It was exhilarating for a girl to arrive at a party in a smart, red, sports car, even though, nine times out of ten, Jamie would find himself abandoned once the party was under way. Boys who had barely spoken to him at school were now eager to join him on Saturday afternoon drives down the south coast or Sunday jaunts to the beaches up north. No one else had a car like Jamie's and he knew perfectly well that the ownership of such an object gave him a power over his peers that he had never enjoyed before. He made the most of it. And he never made the mistake of allowing anyone else to drive the car. He did not delude himself. He wished, with all his heart, that he could be granted social acceptance for his own sake, but it was obvious to him that he was tolerated largely because of the car. The car and the money. Walter was overly generous and made sure that Jamie had sufficient funds to pay for outings with friends. So Jamie received regular invitations for Friday and Saturday nights because he could be relied on, not only to drive his friends to their chosen destination, but also to pay the expenses of anyone who happened to be short of cash on the night. Jamie knew he was being used but he believed that if he were given sufficient opportunities to join in normal social activities then it would only be a matter of time before he was accepted for himself. Surely one of the girls he drove around in his car would appreciate his true value and offer him real friendship and understanding. He did not contemplate turning to prostitutes for sexual release. He was waiting for love to come and save him.

One day, a few months after Jamie's twenty-first birthday, a girl came into the Elizabeth Bay coffee lounge and asked for a job as a waitress. Walter was reluctant to take her on because he liked his waitresses to exude self-confidence and to have a sophisticated, worldly air, whereas this girl looked so shy, so subdued and so innocent that he didn't think she'd do for his kind of establishment.

'What experience have you had?' he wanted to know.

'Well, I've worked in our milk bar in Dubbo,' she said. 'That's where I come from. We serve meals there as well. I'm good at remembering orders.'

'We get so busy here,' said Walter. 'I don't think you've had the kind of experience I need.'

'Please, Mister, I'll learn quickly. Really I will,' and her large blue eyes filled with tears. 'I've got to get a job. I've got to get one today. I've come down from Dubbo, you see, because I just can't live there any longer. And I've got hardly any money.'

Jamie felt such empathy for the girl that he butted in. 'Give her a job, Dad. You can see she really needs it,' he said.

'You'll have to do something with your hair,' said Walter. 'I can't have a waitress with a ponytail. You look like a schoolgirl. And you need a bit of lipstick. Get one of the other girls to show you how to use eye make-up, will you?'

'I'll do anything, anything, if you'll just give me a job,' she said.

'Where are you staying?' Jamie asked her.

'Nowhere yet. I thought I'd better get a job first,' she replied.

'Have you got any money? How are you going to pay for a room?' Jamie wanted to know.

And the girl burst into heartfelt sobs. She wept so profusely that both Walter and Jamie were embarrassed by her outburst. 'I just had to get away. It was my stepfather, you see. He kept getting drunk and hitting my mother. I couldn't stand it any longer so I left.'

Further questioning revealed that the girl's name was Linda, that she was eighteen years old and that she did not have enough money to pay for a room or food. By now Walter shared Jamie's sympathy and felt bound to help the girl.

'Look,' he said, 'I usually pay my waitresses at the end of every fortnight but I'll give you two weeks' wages now and I'll keep paying you in advance. Go and get yourself somewhere to stay and come back tomorrow morning to start work.'

'Thank you, oh thank you, Mister.'

'Liebler, Mr Liebler. And this is my son, Jamie.'

'I promise I'll work really hard. You won't regret taking me on, honestly you won't.'

And Walter did not regret giving Linda a job, not because she turned out to be a good waitress (she was only average in the performance of her duties) but because she was so willing and eager to become Jamie's friend. Whenever she saw Jamie her eyes lit up with genuine pleasure and it seemed to Walter that she did not even notice his deformities. Within a week Jamie and Linda were spending all their spare time together.

Linda was naive, guileless and entirely without malice. She was the kind of person who felt drawn to the lame and helpless. She certainly noticed that Jamie's build and gait were abnormal, that his knuckles and wrists were swollen and misshapen, that his breath was often short and sharp as a consequence of intense pain, but these problems made her heart swell in sympathy and she was not repelled by his abnormalities. Her hand would have reached out to help any disadvantaged creature so the fact that he had something physically wrong with him actually increased his worthiness in her eyes. She was alone in the city. She knew no one; so he took her over, introduced her to his friends, took her to parties and movies, for car rides and ferry rides. As far as she was concerned, Jamie was good and kind and generous. 'Poor boy,' she thought, 'he needs affection so badly.' And she proceeded to give him the thing that he craved.

They would drive off to secluded parking spots almost every night, steam up the windows, take off their clothes and make love to each other. There was an innocence in their love making because she refused to go all the way. Any amount of petting, kissing and mutual masturbation was permitted but no penetration. Jamie didn't mind. To feel her marvellous, yielding flesh next to his was nothing short of ecstasy.

He told her that he loved her, adored her. 'I feel like a lost gem in an uncut stone,' he said, 'and you have discovered me and allowed me to shine through from my stony prison.' When he talked like that Linda didn't quite know what to say. It was embarrassing. 'Will you marry me, Linda? Please say you'll marry me,' he begged.

'I'm too young to think about getting married,' said Linda. She felt terribly sorry for him and she really liked being with him but she was sensible enough to realise that sympathy was not a sound basis for marriage. 'Ask me again when I'm twenty-one,' she said. 'I'm not even going to think about it until then.' She didn't want to offend him and this seemed the best way to put him off for the moment. She did not dismiss the possibility of growing to love him but she was disturbed by the intensity of his desperate need for reassurance.

Indeed, it was this hunger for acceptance that most people found difficult to tolerate. To see such a raw necessity in the eyes of another is a reminder of how despairing loneliness can be. Jamie tried, of course, in his association with others, to behave as they behaved in the hope that he would be admitted to their circle as an equal. But he could never quite achieve his purpose. He tried too hard and the result was that he accentuated, rather than lessened, his difference and he alienated others, rather than winning their favour. No one wants to be reminded constantly of another's naked need.

Jamie thought that having a girlfriend would, at last, raise his value in the eyes of his friends but that was not so. Now that he spent so much time with Linda, he was no longer available as a chauffeur, and the money he had willingly parted with to subsidise his poorer friends, was now spent on Linda. It was not long before invitations to parties and outings ceased altogether. He was hurt by this rejection but not as deeply as he might have been because he did, after all, have Linda and being with Linda was the thing he wanted most in the world.

'We don't need anyone else, except each other,' he declared to Linda. 'When two people really love each other they make a world of their own. A perfect world. Don't you feel that, Linda? Don't you think that's true about you and me? When we're together, we're safe. No one can hurt us. All we have to do is love each other, forever and ever.'

'It mightn't be as simple as that, Jamie,' said Linda. 'I really like being with you. You know that. But I don't know about love. My mother loved my stepfather when she first met him. She thought they'd love each other forever but he ended up being mean and cruel to her. People can change, you know. They don't always stay the same.'

'I'll never change,' said Jamie. 'I'll always love you. In fifty years' time I'll love you just as much as I do now.'

'I don't want to think about forever. It gives me the creeps thinking that far ahead. We're having fun now, aren't we? Let's just enjoy ourselves. I wish you'd stop talking about the future all the time.' But it was difficult for Jamie to do as she asked because his driving need was to secure a guarantee of continuing affection.

Three months later, when he least expected it, Jamie suffered an arthritic attack so severe that he had to be taken to hospital. They had all become complacent, assuming that, since he had been free of acute episodes for nine years, the disease might have run its course. Even the doctors had been optimistic. Walter and Elizabeth, and Jamie himself, had certainly, over the years, turned hope into belief and belief into the conviction that no further deterioration would occur. They were all shocked by the vicious nature of this latest assault. It seemed that every joint in his body was inflamed and swollen so that he lay in agony, involuntarily screaming with the pain and weeping with rage at the unfairness of it all. Why now? Now, when he had found love, when he had begun to hope for future happiness. Why? Why? Why? And this time the attack had sinister implications. Severe chest pains indicated that cardiac lesions had occurred. Now that the heart muscle was involved the doctors could not rule out the possibility of early death from heart failure.

Jamie's illness brought Walter and Elizabeth together in a concerted effort to win Linda's approval and to persuade her that it would be worth her while to continue with the relationship. They drove her to the hospital to visit Jamie; they took her out for dinner, bought her clothes and jewellery, promised a house, a car and financial security forever if she would stay with Jamie and become his wife. She was not swayed by such promises but continued to visit Jamie for several months because she cared for him and because she felt sorry for him. However, Jamie's condition did not change. He showed no improvement and, in the end, it was more than she could bear. She told Elizabeth that she could not go on and she told Walter that she would have to stop working for him. She wrote Jamie a letter.

Dear Jamie,

I'm sorry but I'll have to go away. I can't stay with you because I can't stand to see you in so much pain.

With love,

Linda

Jamie was at first inconsolable but he did not see Linda's departure as defection. His pain was so great, his illness so severe that he understood her leaving. He could hardly bear to go on himself, let alone expect her to go on with him. He thought about their love and it seemed to him that their relationship had been like a fast, exhilarating drive on a country road. And now, quite suddenly, their love had met an obstacle so great that they could go no further. He was consumed with sadness and loneliness. He believed, however, that he had loved and been loved. There was all the difference in the world between losing love and never having been loved at all.

As the months dragged by, Jamie became more and more difficult as a patient. He shouted at the nurses if his needs were not met immediately, abused the doctors and accused them of not knowing what they were doing, demanded higher and higher doses of pain killers and, occasionally, hurled trays of food on the floor if he found the hospital meals unacceptable. Elizabeth brought him food from home but he always found fault with it. Walter brought him strawberries but they were the wrong colour and lobsters but they were the wrong size. He remained rigid and uncooperative during his daily physiotherapy sessions while the poor therapist struggled to put his joints through their normal range of movement by means of gentle therapeutic exercises. Even though hot baths and hot compresses were used before the exercises, in order to diminish pain and muscle spasm, Jamie continued to complain of unbearable pain. He felt that he was being tortured rather than helped. 'Gutter splints' were made for his legs. These long, leg cylinder casts were used at night to immobilise his inflamed and painful hip and knee joints and wrist splints were provided to ease the pain in his hands.

It was fourteen months before the inflammation came under control and by then Jamie's knee joints had suffered such serious deterioration that he could not walk without crutches. The doctors recommended knee replacements. With new, artificial knee joints he might be able to walk again unaided. He would certainly be able to get around using canes or sticks rather than crutches. Although the operations would be time consuming and debilitating Jamie wanted to have them done. The idea of spending the rest of his life as a real cripple was too horrific to contemplate. Four months and two operations later, Jamie was moved to a rehabilitation centre. He was to spend six months there, learning to walk on his new knees.

At the rehabilitation centre Jamie found the courage to go on because he was thrown among people who were worse off than he was. There were victims of shocking car accidents, so mutilated and damaged that Jamie wondered how anyone could believe that any kind of rehabilitation would be possible. There were paraplegics and quadriplegics and patients who had been so badly burned that their features were unrecognisable. Yet here they were, all trying their best to take one small step towards recovery. The doctors, nurses and therapists exuded an air of quiet determination. This was a place where results were achieved against impossible odds and if there were days when Jamie felt depressed and despondent then he learned to keep his despair to himself.

There was a pastor connected to the centre and although Jamie had rejected the approaches of ministers of various faiths during his stay in hospital, he found this pastor particularly easy to talk to. He simply walked around chatting to people, offering words of encouragement and support. He talked about the courageous spirit of man and only occasionally mentioned the fact that God could help people during their times of difficulty.

'I don't believe in God, you know,' said Jamie. 'How can I? If I believed in God I'd have to believe he was a cruel God. Look what he's done to me! If I believed in God I'd have to hate him and I've decided it's better not to believe at all than to hate.'

'You're angry, James,' said the pastor. 'You're asking, "Why me? Why do I have to suffer?" Look at all these poor people around you. Why you? Why them? Perhaps God has sent these trials to each of you as a means of helping you to grow strong. True love, true humanity, is found through suffering. Your suffering makes you special in God's eyes. Believe me, you'll emerge from this experience as a better person with a compassionate spirit and a loving soul.'

Jamie could not accept the pastor's notion of God but he was attracted to the idea of spiritual existence. He did believe that he had a soul and he believed that his soul was a precious thing of great beauty. The idea that physical existence and physical suffering were meaningless when compared to the spiritual power of the soul was something to hold onto and the thought of his soul, struggling through his present predicament, until it transcended the confines of his body, was a source of comfort to him.

There was a small, dark, Jewish girl at the centre. Her name was Esther and Jamie became her friend. She was frail, withdrawn and shy. She suffered from an inoperable, faulty heart valve and Jamie was very surprised to learn that she was actually twenty-three years old, a few months older than himself. She looked like a child. Her parents were delighted when Jamie made friends with her. They visited her frequently and, as Elizabeth was a daily visitor, the parents soon developed a rapport. Walter became involved and the girl's parents began to plot a viable future for their daughter.

Our girl. Your boy. Neither of them have any chance of marrying into the normal world. Why not arrange a marriage between them? It was a perfect solution, wasn't it? It seemed like a good idea to Walter. Elizabeth was not so sure but the girl's parents pressed and Elizabeth agreed to discuss the matter with Jamie.

'How do you feel about Esther, James?' Elizabeth asked, as she and Jamie went for a slow walk in the garden of the rehabilitation centre. Jamie was progressing well, still using canes but walking almost normally.

'Esther? She's a nice girl. We're friends. What do you mean?'

'I wondered if you felt more than friendship for her,' said Elizabeth, 'because her parents have approached us. They'd like you to marry Esther.'

'Marry Esther? Mum, Esther will be dead in two or three years. You know that as well as I do. How could you think I'd want to marry her?'

'Her parents ….. your father ….. I suppose even I thought it might be some comfort to you to marry,' said Elizabeth.

'Is that how you think of me? You want to lump me in together with a misfit of a girl who's going to die? Is that how you see me?'

'No, James, that's not how I see you,' said Elizabeth.

'She's got a skinny, childish body and she's going to die! There's nothing about Esther that attracts me. If I ever get married it's going to be to someone who's normal. I'm not going to settle for some poor, pathetic creature that no one else wants!' And Jamie was so furious that he turned his back on his mother and walked away.

Six weeks later Jamie was allowed to return home. He did not know what he was going to do with the rest of his life but he was determined to find a path to follow that would be in accord with his own vision of himself. He felt an inner strength. He would not be ruled by either of his parents. He told his father that he would not be returning to work with him. Coffee lounges did not interest him. Walter accepted the decision, largely because he did not believe that Jamie would ever be well enough to work again. Elizabeth did not share this pessimistic view. She offered Jamie her wholehearted support in anything he decided to do. The months in the rehabilitation centre had inspired Jamie. He was going to live his own life and live it in his own way.

CHAPTER 3

Jamie's first step towards beginning a life of his own was to go to a large city stationary store and buy himself the most beautiful notebook he could find. The one he chose was large and thick with a light grey, marble-patterned cover. The pages were creamy smooth with faint, green lines. He did not intend keeping a diary but rather a journal recording significant moments of insight. He had thoughts and ideas that he would like to convey to others and writing them down would be a first step in fulfilling that ambition. He understood the nature of his illness and knew that he could not expect to live a normal lifespan. There was something dramatic and tragic about imagining his own early death. His mother would find the journal. She would read it and give it to others to read. His words would be published. The entire world would know of his suffering. Everyone would recognise the true, inner beauty of his soul and he would live forever in the minds and hearts of others.

So Jamie took his beautiful new notebook into his room, locked the door to assure himself of privacy, took out a fine black biro and printed neatly on the first page.

'Dedicated to my mother, whose love made these writings possible.'

He hesitated for a few moments. He wasn't sure how to go on but he turned the page, put the date at the top right-hand corner and sat there expectantly, pen poised, waiting for words and images to spill onto the page.

How he wished he could exist in mind only and be free of the crippled body sitting at the desk. He thought of his poor mother. How cruel he'd been to her during this last, long stay in hospital. She'd come to see him every day, brought him food from home. It was difficult to forgive himself for being so rude to her but then he'd been angry at being stuck in there, month after month, while she was free to come and go at will. And yet she hadn't reproached him. She'd understood that the love she brought was not the kind he needed. It was Linda's love he'd needed and Linda had left him. At the time he'd been able to rationalise her departure but now, in retrospect, he realised that she couldn't have loved him. If she'd really loved him then she'd have stuck by him, wouldn't she? If anything terrible had happened to her, if she'd been maimed in an accident or burnt in a fire, he'd still have loved her.

No more Linda. No more love. How faithless women were. He was not going to let himself be hurt again. Women could be observed, appreciated aesthetically but never touched again. There'd been a young nurse at the hospital, tranquil and composed, poised and pretty. Her quiet, infectious smile had radiated like ripples on a pond. He would have been content if he could have picked her up and held her in the palm of his hand, like a priceless pearl, to gaze on her beauty, for beauty's sake, forever.

The pursuit of beauty. That's something his father knew nothing about. So rooted in the real world of business and money, sport and sex. And yet his father must, at one time, have seen beauty in his mother. Such a sweet face she had. That soft, gentle smile. But his father had discarded her like a piece of dirty linen. She should have found another man to love. Was it Jamie's fault that she was still alone? Was she so loyal to her son that she couldn't allow herself to love another? The thought of his father's defection still aroused anger and resentment. Walter's world must be rejected. Jamie would turn his back on the material world. Beauty of the soul, beauty of the spirit - these were the paths he must follow.

Jamie's decision to give up the world of the flesh in favour of the world of the spirit brought with it a sense of superiority and a glow of righteousness but the pen still remained poised in his hand and the page remained blank. With a sigh of disappointment he closed his notebook and put it away. Perhaps he would be able to write another day.

Jamie discussed possible career paths with his old school friend, Judy. Judy had never wavered in her friendship, not since the day she had taken him under her wing during their first week at high school. Judy was still too tall and gawky to be regarded as attractive to men but she was making the best of her life. She had completed a Science degree and had spent the last two years travelling and working overseas. She'd returned only recently and was employed as a microbiologist in a large city hospital. She'd been distressed to learn how ill Jamie had been during her absence and was now trying to make up for her lack of support over this period of time by helping him to find something meaningful to do with his life.

'I want to be an artist of some kind,' he told her. 'I don't want to lead a mainstream life. I don't want a wife and children and a mortgage. I want my spirit to be free. And I want to associate with people who are looking for an alternative lifestyle, a way of life that isn't bound by conventions, a communal sort of life devoted to beauty and to art. I wouldn't care if I starved in a garret as long as I was happy in what I was doing.'

'Don't you have any ideas about what sort of artist you want to be?' Judy asked.

'Well, at first I thought about being a writer but it's hard to get started,' said Jamie.

'I don't think writing is a good idea, James. Not as a career. It's so isolating. It would be better for you to do a course of some kind. You'd meet people that way, make new friends. Why don't we go out to East Sydney Technical College? They run all sorts of art courses there.'

The Information Officer at the college was very helpful, providing Jamie with outlines of several courses and suggesting that, if he were interested, he could attend a series of exhibition nights that were scheduled to take place in a few weeks' time. It was now mid-November and the final year students in each discipline would be staging an end of course display of their work in graphics, painting and pottery.

Judy accompanied Jamie to the pottery night and witnessed his transformation. Not only were the beautiful end products displayed but the students demonstrated the entire process of pottery making. When Jamie first saw a girl, sitting at a wheel, head bent in concentration, muddy hands dripping with water as she turned a ball of clay into an exquisitely formed vase, he knew instantly that this was what he had to do. His hands longed to plunge into the wet, muddy clay. He could almost feel the sensuous ooze of the clay between his fingers. He knew that this was the way, the only way, for him to create objects of beauty.

Getting into the course was no easy matter. He made an appointment to see the Head Teacher and was told that successful acceptance rested on a body of submitted work. Applicants were expected to have completed part-time courses or to have done pottery as their major work while studying Art at high school. They could only take twenty-four full-time students. They always had many more applications than places. They were committed, therefore, to taking the most promising students. The course was demanding. Three years full-time study. They had to be sure they chose the right applicants, those who would last the distance. Jamie begged and pleaded. He had never done pottery in his life. He had no work to submit. But he knew that this was what he had to do. This was his destiny. He must be allowed to do the course.

The Head Teacher had, of course, already taken note of Jamie's disabilities. On this particular day it had been necessary for Jamie to use his metal walking sticks and the abnormality of his wrists and finger joints were quite obvious to the teacher. Yet the boy burned with such intense enthusiasm that the Head Teacher was reluctant to turn him away.

'I'll tell you something, James. Technical colleges now have a policy of helping the disadvantaged. I'm only supposed to have twenty-four students in the course but if I made a submission on your behalf, as a physically disabled student, I'd be able to increase the class size to twenty-five.'

'But I don't want to be treated as a cripple,' said James.

'You won't be treated as a cripple but unless you allow me to use your physical disabilities as a means of getting you into the course, you have no chance,' said the Head Teacher.

'But if I do get into the course I don't want any special concessions. I want to be on the same footing as everyone else,' said Jamie.

'James, you'll be starting at a disadvantage. Don't imagine for one moment that it will be easy for you and don't be so pig-headed that you refuse extra help when it's offered to you. Believe me, you're going to need it.'

'Then you'll let me do the course?'

'I'll make my submission. I'll do my best for you.'

Three weeks later Jamie received a letter granting him special permission to enrol. He was asked to submit a doctor's report outlining the full extent of his physical disabilities so that his disadvantages could be taken into account in assessing his performance. He had not told his mother or his father of his application. He wanted to wait until he was certain of acceptance before saying anything. Elizabeth was delighted but Walter was furious.

'Pottery? Pottery? That's for women. Men don't do courses in pottery,' said Walter.

'You're so prejudiced, Dad. You don't know what you're talking about. The Head Teacher is a man,' said Jamie.

'I bet he's a poofter,' said Walter. 'Real men don't do pottery.'

'Then maybe, Dad, I'm not a real man. Not in your terms. But I've got into this course and it was very difficult to get into and I'm going to do it, whether you like it or not,' said Jamie.

'If you want to do some course, then why don't you do something useful? Something like accountancy. If you did an accountancy course you could do all the books for my business. You could be really helpful. Earn a decent living,' said Walter.

'I don't want to be an accountant, Dad. I want to be a potter. An artist. And I'm going to make a living at it, believe me. The course isn't expensive. It won't cost you much. I just need to know that you'll keep supporting me financially while I do it.'

Walter was insulted. 'Do you think I'd ever let you down?' When he said that his voice broke a little and there were tears in the corner of his eyes. 'I just want you to be happy, Jamie, that's all.'

'I am happy, Dad. I'll be doing something that I really want to do,' said Jamie.

'That's alright then,' said Walter.

Jamie had six or seven weeks to wait until the course began in mid-February and he didn't want to waste time. He went to the local library and borrowed several books on pottery, studying the process, learning the correct terms, writing reference notes for himself. He contacted several community centres that ran part-time pottery courses, hoping that he might be able to do a short, introductory course, but they were all closing down for the long Christmas holidays. However one of the people he spoke to gave him the name of a woman potter in Balmain who might be able to help him. She was very kind when he rang her. She was going on holidays until mid-January but she agreed to allow him to come to her studio as often as he liked after that. He spent four weeks with her, observing all she did. As she worked, she talked, telling Jamie all she knew and always explaining how she felt about each step of the process. She let him help her with the easier tasks, like applying the first glaze and packing the kiln. When he met his classmates for the first time he wanted to know as much about pottery as they did. Jamie had never been happier.

Walter had, in a sense, been correct in that a majority of Jamie's fellow students were female. In the class of twenty-five, only eight were male and a few of these were clearly homosexual. Jamie, who had recently turned twenty-four, had worried that he might be older than the other students but this was not so. Some of the students had come to the course straight from school but the majority were as old, or older than Jamie. This was particularly true of the women, several of whom were in their thirties. When they looked each other over on that first day, Jamie was well aware of eyes that stared, then glanced away. His longing for acceptance was as great as it had been on his first day of high school.

If Jamie's classmates initially thought that he had been admitted to the course by special dispensation, this idea was quickly dispelled by the superior technical knowledge he displayed. The problem was that he was too eager to display it. He tried to answer every question before anyone else and he took every opportunity that arose to show off what he knew. Within a few days his eagerness to please was irritating certain members of the class, particularly the younger ones. The mature, older students were more tolerant, taking Jamie's behaviour for what it was - the overwhelming need of a crippled boy to find favour with his peers.

On the practical side, it was clear from the beginning that Jamie was having difficulties. When he first tried to cut off a piece of clay, he did not have enough strength in his hands to get the cutting wire right through the block. To his great embarrassment the teacher came over and spoke to him quietly.

'Here, James, let me give you a hand with that.' Jamie hoped no one had noticed that he needed help but he was sure that the eyes of every member of the class were on him.

Learning how to wedge the clay to get rid of air bubbles was almost impossible until he realised that it required coordination rather than strength. Standing at the hard wooden bench, kneading the clay, holding and pushing. Hour after hour he stood there, attempting to master the technique. And the wheel! It looked so easy when used by an expert. There was so much to think of, so many aspects to coordinate. First the wheel had to be dampened, the ball of clay thrown onto the centre, the left elbow on the hip, the right hand pushing down on the clay, the hole made in the centre with the thumb, the clay grabbed underneath and pushed up to cone the walls. You had to do it over and over again to get it right. You needed to have a visual image of what you wanted to make but the thing you actually produced never seemed to quite correspond to your vision. And you needed to keep adding water to the clay. The only pleasure in the whole process was the soothing feeling of the milky film of water running through your fingers. When you worked the wheel your back ached and your wrists ached and your arms ached but you kept going because you knew you weren't the only person who found this difficult. The wheel was a skill to be mastered and, in the early stages of the course, there was not one student in the class who had yet achieved that mastery.

Jamie knew that it was going to take him longer than anyone else so he came to college early in the morning and stayed after everyone had left in the afternoon. Even those who found some aspects of Jamie's behaviour difficult to take could not help but admire his effort to overcome his physical disadvantages. Day after day he put in the extra hours of practice, determined that he would not fall behind. He willed himself to ignore his physical pain as he concentrated his attention on the task of learning these new, necessary skills. When he got into his car to drive home he was close to collapse but he knew he was improving and that was enough to keep him going. After dinner at night he took painkillers and sleeping pills and sank into exhausted sleep.

In comparison to the work on the wheel, the days of decorating were easy. Using the small, rotating, metal wheel, painting his designs onto a finished plate or bowl or cup, applying the last, creative touches before the second firing in the kiln - these activities were sheer joy. Although he preferred decorating pottery to making it, he knew that total satisfaction was only possible because he had undertaken every step of the process. Difficult and demanding though the work was, by the end of the first year of the course he knew that he was going to make it.

The euphoria that accompanied the successful completion of a year's hard work soon gave way to depression. Jamie spent many hours lying on his bed, thinking about his achievements of the last twelve months but always, in the end, sinking into morbid self-pity. He contemplated his weakness, his twisted body, his painful flesh and bones. He could not bear to be alone! He might have been able to endure his isolation if it were not necessary to live in such close physical proximity to others. Even when he was walking down the street he wanted to reach out and touch perfect strangers who passed him by. How he longed for the warm breath, the soft caress of some other human being. Vowing that he would live a celibate life and devote himself to art was all very well in theory but it did not work in practice. He could put his heart and soul into making beautiful pieces of pottery but that did not mean that he could live without love. His soul was trapped in a monstrous body. Would no one ever set it free?

On New Year's Eve Jamie felt severe chest pains and was hospitalised once again. Cardiac arrest was feared but the pains subsided almost immediately and he was allowed to go home after a week. His doctors gave him a strict lecture. He was taking too many painkillers. He must, of course, continue with the anti-inflammatory medication but he had to reduce his intake of strong analgesics and take sleeping pills only occasionally. He must remember that he had irreparable heart lesions. If he continued to use dangerous drugs indiscriminately then he was reducing his chance of long-term survival.

Jamie felt angry. What did these doctors know? How could they gauge the extent of his pain or his agonising need for sleep? He would do as he pleased and take drugs according to his own assessment of his own needs. He did, however, agree to spend the next six weeks convalescing. His mother rented a cottage at Hawk's Nest. They swam and sunbaked, read books and rested, and Elizabeth, who had become a fanatical bridge player, decided to occupy Jamie's mind by teaching him how to play. By the end of their holiday Jamie had, in fact, reduced his medication dramatically and had gathered his strength in preparation for the year to come.

Jamie had won his place in the class and was therefore free of the anxiety associated with the need to prove his worth. He was more relaxed, more natural with his classmates and they responded by treating him as an equal in the classroom. He worked beside Jessica, a woman in her late thirties, and he found her presence both peaceful and calming. She was always alert to his difficulties and particularly sensitive to his periods of intense pain. 'Just rest a moment, James,' she might say to him. 'This isn't a race. There's no prize for finishing first,' and her generous mouth would bestow on him a wide, sympathetic smile. Everything about Jessica was generous. Her ample breasts and broad hips swayed loosely beneath her long, flowing cotton dresses and she walked with a slow, self-contained, sensual gait. Her grey eyes gazed quietly from a serene oval face. Her skin was sun-tanned and she wore no make-up. She gave the impression of being totally at ease with her own body.

About two weeks after term began, Jessica surprised Jamie by asking him if he were free that afternoon after classes finished. She'd like him to drive her home; there was something she wanted to discuss with him. Perhaps he'd like to stay on for dinner. This was the first time that any of his fellow students had invited him to participate in a social activity outside of the classroom and his heart filled with joy and gratitude. Of course he was free. He'd be delighted to drive her home and he'd love to stay for dinner.

Jamie knew that Jessica lived in a shared house in Kensington, close to the college. He knew that because he'd overheard snippets of conversation between Jessica and two other boys in the class, Sean and Michael. It was clear that Sean and Michael lived in her house and that sometimes they needed to refer to domestic details that concerned all three of them. It was difficult for Jamie to contain his eager anticipation for the rest of the day. Why had she invited him? What could it be that she wanted to discuss with him?

When they arrived at the house, Jamie was amazed at its size. It was a single-storeyed house but it had five bedrooms, a large lounge room and a huge kitchen that was obviously the hub of the house. A round, wooden table, with six chairs, fitted easily at its centre. Jessica led him around the house, showing him all the rooms, leaving her own room for last.

'Come into my room, James, while we have a talk,' she said. The room was quite dark, the windows draped with rich, cotton wall hangings. She did not turn on the light but lit three or four candles, strategically placed around the room. When the candles were lit they cast shadows on the walls. Jamie and Jessica were immediately enclosed in a shadowy, comforting glow. She told him to sit down and, as he did so, he looked about the room. The room affected him profoundly. It was so unusual and it gave the impression of having been furnished with care and commitment. The books were not there for show. Several of them lay open, ready to be perused at any time and the paintings on the walls pulsated in the dim light. They were there for the sole purpose of pleasing her, not for the prying eyes of others. The small table and chairs, the sofa bed with its exotic Indian cover, were chosen as extensions of Jessica's personality. It was a room that belonged absolutely to its occupant. Jamie felt that he, also, could belong in such a room. The chair he sat in was so comfortable that it could have been his very own. He wanted to stay in the room with Jessica forever, silently absorbing its ambience.

'I was wondering, James, if you would like to move into the house. One of the girls who lives here is moving out next week. I need another person to share. I run the house, hold the lease, manage the money for the rent, telephone, electricity and gas. I tend to be a bit bossy. I draw up housework rosters and I expect people to pull their weight. I've lived in communal houses before and I've found that things can get out of hand unless one person takes on the overall responsibility. Apart from a few rules like always washing up your dirty dishes and being considerate of others, everyone is free to do as they please. I choose the people I want to live with. I think you'd fit into our household rather well.'

'Yes,' he said. 'Yes. Yes. Yes. I can't think of anything I'd like better than moving into your house.'

As Jamie drove home his heart expanded with sheer joy and he was so excited that his face kept breaking into involuntary smiles. To be asked! To actually be asked to go and live in Jessica's house! Acceptance. True acceptance at last. He had waited so long for a sign, a gesture, an indication that others were willing to treat him as a social equal. Although he'd said 'Yes', he knew that he could not move in without his parents' approval. Walter gave him a weekly allowance that adequately covered his pocket money and car expenses but he did not have enough to pay for rent and food. His parents would have to be persuaded that leaving home was a necessary and desirable step at this time in his life. He was, after all, twenty-four years old.

'I'm worried, James, naturally,' said Elizabeth. 'I've always felt it was my responsibility to keep an eye on you, make sure you don't over-tire yourself. But I want you to be as independent as possible. Although I don't like it, I think you should leave home. But it's your father you're going to have to convince. He's the one who'll have to provide you with the money.'

Jamie knew that his father would agree but he also knew that he would have to beg and plead and listen to objections before that agreement was secured. Walter, of course, came up with predictable arguments. 'Why should I pay for you to live somewhere when I'm already providing you with a perfectly comfortable home? Who's going to monitor your health and your medication if you stop living with your mother? Why would you want to live with a bunch of people you hardly even know?'

Jamie hated being financially dependent on his father but when he looked at Walter's lifestyle, at the money he lavished on Zelda and Katie for regular holidays overseas, expensive clothes and private school fees, he felt he was only asking for what was due to him. He deserved to be supported and told his father so. After a certain amount of grumbling Walter agreed.

Communal living fell short of Jamie's expectations. He thought the members of the household would pool their food money, shop together, cook together, talk together every evening and, in general, live like a closely knit, harmonious family. It wasn't quite like that. Not in this household. Though some basics like bread, milk, tea, coffee, toilet paper, soap and cleaning materials were paid for from a kitty, Jessica had decided that the joint purchase of food only led to arguments and accusations of unfairness concerning the amount of food particular people consumed. Within the household, however, alliances had been formed. Sean and Michael shared everything, including a bed, although their possessions were spread over two of the bedrooms. Jessica had an arrangement with Wendy, the girl who occupied the fifth bedroom, that they each would shop and cook for the other once a week. After consultation they agreed to extend this arrangement to include Jamie so that three nights a week he could be certain of company for dinner and he was required to provide the food and cook it on only one of the three nights.

These evenings sustained him but there were another four nights in the week and he found that living in a house full of people could, in fact, be quite lonely. He was not used to looking after himself and the whole business of thinking about changing his sheets, washing his clothes and cooking for himself quickly lost its initial glamour. He soon fell into the habit of visiting his mother two nights a week for nourishing meals, taking his dirty washing along with him. Sunday lunch at Walter's, which had become spasmodic, somehow seemed more attractive to Jamie and he became a much more regular attender.

He was, however, intrigued by those who shared the house and sought their company in an endeavour to entrench himself in some way into their lives. His efforts met with partial success but often when he thought he was making some headway, he would find himself being rebuffed. Sean and Michael were prepared to let him enter conversations concerning their homosexuality. They told Jamie that they found it safer to hide their sexual orientation from the outside world. They had short, neatly cropped hair, were clean-shaven and dressed conventionally in jeans and T-shirts. Sean was short, dark-haired, well built and very handsome. If he were alone, no one would have suspected he was gay but Michael was not so fortunate. His willowy build, fair complexion, delicate features and the occasional effeminate gesture gave him away. They were often hurt or upset by particular acts of homophobic prejudice in their daily lives and sometimes brought their despair to the kitchen table. Jamie would listen, with attention and sympathy and then might make a comment.

'I do understand how you feel. I know what it's like to be the victim of prejudice because you're different from others.' But they did not want to recognise Jamie as a fellow member of a minority group. They saw no parallels between his situation and their own and dismissed his attempts to forge a sympathetic link on the basis of similarity. There was a strong bond, however, because of their mutual desire to eventually earn their living as potters and many hours were spent discussing how this might be achieved. Sean and Michael were keen to set up a cooperative when they had completed the course and they asked Jamie if he'd be interested in joining them. It would take money to get started, to rent premises, set up a studio with all the equipment they would need and establish a retail outlet for their work.

'I'll get the money,' said Jamie. 'My dad always complains but he usually gives me what I want. I'm sure I can talk him into it when the time comes.' Jamie did not suspect that Sean and Michael pretended a greater friendship for him than they actually felt because they realised he came from a financially comfortable family. He saw them as genuine friends, even when they went off to the movies without asking him to join them. They were, after all, a sexual couple. Perhaps they felt some need to go to the movies alone.

It was the sexuality in the house that Jamie found disturbing because he was excluded and deprived. Jessica frequently entertained men in her room. At first, Jamie was shocked and surprised by the variety and the number of her lovers.

'Love is something I reserve for my work,' she said. 'All my feelings and emotions go into my art. The pots I create are my children. I can't afford to become involved with any man. But I like sex. It's necessary for my health and well-being. I'm an earth mother, really. I love to give myself physically, sexually. But I keep my spirit intact. My soul belongs to myself alone. That's why I enjoy having different lovers. There are no complications that way.'

'That's alright for you,' said Jamie. 'I'd like to have that kind of philosophy. But it wouldn't do me much good, would it? There's no great line of women waiting out there to sleep with me.'

'Oh, James, I'm sorry. I'd offer to sleep with you but it wouldn't be a good idea. I have one very definite rule for myself. I don't have sex with anyone living in the house. It only leads to complications. You can see that, can't you?'

'You couldn't make an exception to the rule, could you? Just for me?' He said this in a rueful, joking kind of way.

'I'm sorry, James. Anyway, I should be honest with you. If I had sex with you it would be out of pity, not out of desire.'

'Thanks for reminding me of how unattractive I am,' said Jamie.

'No, James, that's not true. You're not attractive to me but there could easily be other women who would find you very appealing,' said Jessica.

'I don't think so.' And Jamie wandered back to his room, feeling very sorry for himself. He tried to ignore the sexuality in the house but it was difficult to do so. Any murmur or sound that came from the room Sean and Michael shared seemed to carry a hint of lovemaking while the cries of Jessica's throaty orgasms reverberated through the house. As the months passed and Jamie settled in, he felt that he understood his fellow occupants fairly well. Except for Wendy, that is. Wendy remained an enigma.

Wendy was the only person in the house who was not doing the pottery course and Jamie knew nothing about her when he moved in. Six months later he still did not know her at all, despite the fact that they ate dinner together three nights a week. Wendy did not enter conversations. She exchanged pleasantries, was always polite but contributed nothing to the discussions on art, politics, morality and sexuality that were sometimes fiercely debated at the kitchen table. She had answered an advertisement that Jessica had put in the local paper when she'd first set up the household. Jessica had to admit that eighteen months of communal living had given her no clue as to Wendy's inner thoughts and feelings. Even direct questions such as, 'What do you think about free love,

Wendy?' failed to elicit a response. She would smile, in a shy, embarrassed way, get up from the table and say that she would have to go to her room now; she had a great deal of work to get through before tomorrow.

Although Wendy was only twenty-one, she was already a tutor in English Language at the University of NSW. She'd topped her honours year and, as well as tutoring, she had begun her Master of Arts postgraduate work in some obscure aspect of Anglo-Saxon poetry. It was obvious to everyone in the house that she was brilliant, that she would get her M.A. Honours without any trouble and would go on to do a Ph.D. She'd progress from being a tutor to becoming a lecturer and would, no doubt, end up as a professor of English Language at some university either in Australia or overseas. Her devotion to her work seemed to be absolute and Jamie imagined that her unwillingness to discuss her studies was due to the fact that her field of expertise was so specialised that no one would have known what she was talking about.

She was always neat and clean but gave the impression of not caring about her appearance. Her clothes were old-fashioned, demure, childish in their modesty. Her mode of dress and the way she walked were clearly designed to avoid, rather than attract, attention. She was of medium height and slender in build and might have succeeded in avoiding attention altogether were it not for her face and hair. Her light auburn hair fell to her shoulders in a tumble of tiny, riotous curls and framed a face so beautifully structured that one could not help but admire it. High cheekbones, square jaw, small nose, green eyes. Her skin was very pale and her face so arresting that Jamie had blushed and stuttered when first introduced to her. On closer acquaintance, however, she seemed less attractive because her eyes radiated no warmth and her face revealed no emotion. Wendy appeared to be a person for whom intellect was paramount. That her intellect was housed in a body that might have been attractive was obviously unimportant to her.

One night, when Jamie had cooked spaghetti bolognaise for Jessica and Wendy, and Jessica had gone off to entertain her latest lover, Wendy remained seated at the kitchen table rather than following her usual pattern of rushing off to her room as soon as the meal was over. Jamie began to clear the table. His hands were particularly swollen and painful that day and he dropped one of the dishes. When it broke, splattering uneaten meat and tomato sauce over the floor he sat down and wept with anger and frustration.

'Oh, James, let me help you,' Wendy cried.

'No. I'll do it,' said James. He took out a handkerchief, wiped his eyes and tried to get up.

Wendy put a hand on his shoulder. 'Just sit down, will you!' And she started to clear up the mess on the floor.

'But it's my turn tonight,' said Jamie. 'Shopping. Cooking. Cleaning up.'

'Don't be ridiculous, James,' said Wendy and she began to do the washing up. When she'd finished, she came over to the kitchen table and sat down next to him. She reached over and took hold of one of his hands. The taking of the hand was not a gesture of warmth or affection but rather a means of making an examination of the swollen joints, the crooked fingers. When she'd completed her study she put the hand down. She looked up into his face. 'Are you often in pain?' she asked.

'Always,' Jamie replied.

'I didn't realise that.'

'It's a matter of degree, a matter of intensity. Every joint in my body is affected. Something always hurts. But the pain is on the move. Some days it's my fingers, sometimes my ankles or my hips or my elbows or my neck. Sometimes the level of pain is quite manageable. Sometimes it's unbearable,' said Jamie.

'How can you live like that? How can you put up with it?' she asked.

'What choice do I have? This is the only body I've got. I wish I didn't have to live in it. I wish someone would take my mind and my soul and put them into a new body. But that's not going to happen. So I have to make the best of things. And I can't waste time, you see, because bodies like mine obviously don't last too long,' said Jamie.

'You're incredibly strong, James. I do admire you for that. And James, at any time, if the pain really gets so bad that you can't bear it, I wish you'd call me. I'm just in the room next to yours, you know. If you think I could help.' Then she bent over and kissed him on the cheek. She gave his hand a squeeze, got up from the table and went to her room. Jamie remained seated at the kitchen table for quite some time. The touch of her lips on his cheek had made the blood rush through him, banishing all his pain. If only he could have a love such as Wendy for his own. If he could feel her touch every day of his life then surely his body would be soothed and healed.

Nothing changed. Not outwardly. Wendy went on behaving as she had always behaved, as though the intimacy in the kitchen that night had never occurred. But Jamie had changed. He had begun to hope again for love and once he allowed that hope a foothold in his mind it took him over completely. Each night he lay in the bedroom next to Wendy's, burning with desire, longing to feel her lips once again on his cheek, remembering the touch of her hand on his. Should he speak? Should he declare his everlasting love? Should he demand his right to love and be loved before he was swept away to cruel and early death? What if she rejected him? What if she turned to him and said, 'I'm sorry, I can't love you in that way.' That would be the end, wouldn't it? The end of hope. The end of dreams. He'd be left with a soul full of sadness. Better to hope. Better to dream. Better to say nothing.

Jamie usually gave Jessica a lift to college each day and on one particular morning she realised that if he didn't get up soon they were going to be late. She knocked on his door and he managed to find sufficient voice to ask her to come in.

'Something's happened to me, Jessica. I can't move,' he said. 'You'll have to call my doctor for me. The number's in a little pocket diary in the drawer next to my bed. And my mother, you'd better ring her as well.'

The doctor wanted Jamie to go to hospital. 'You have some kind of build up of spinal fluid. That's what's causing the dizziness. A lumbar puncture will relieve the pressure but it's a process that's not without risks. I prefer to do it under sterile conditions in a hospital.'

'I'm not going,' said Jamie. 'I know what'll happen if you get me into hospital. You'll keep me there for months. I want you to do the spinal tap here. If it doesn't work then I'll have to go in but please, please try to help me here at home. I'm doing all I can to lead a normal life.'

When the doctor turned Jamie on his side and inserted the needle at the base of his spine, liquid gushed into the drip tray he was holding. After this initial rush, the fluid slowed to a steady drip and the doctor continued to sit there for a good thirty minutes, until he was satisfied that sufficient fluid had been removed. The relief was instantaneous. When the doctor removed the needle, Jamie was able to turn onto his back unassisted. The dizziness was gone.

'You're not to move today. And rest for the next few days. I'll have this fluid tested to make sure you haven't contracted an infection. Come and see me on Friday. You can't go back to college until next week. Is that understood?' said the doctor.

Elizabeth, who had come over immediately in response to Jessica's call, wanted to take Jamie home with her but he refused. He agreed to allow her to stay and look after him for the rest of the day but Jessica assured her that there would be enough members of the household home that night to get Jamie anything he needed.

Wendy had left the house without knowing that Jamie was ill and when she returned he was rewarded by her sincere distress and concern. Indeed, he was considerably cheered by the response of everyone in the house. Jessica had not gone to college until she was sure Elizabeth could spend the day with Jamie. Sean and Michael had come in, late in the afternoon, to see how he was. They'd sat at the end of his bed for at least forty minutes, chatting to him in a very amicable way. Wendy was cooking that night. She was making her delicious stir-fried chicken with vegetables and rice. As Jamie lay in his bed, the door of his room open, a wonderful aroma of ginger and honey and chilli wafted through from the kitchen. Jamie moved his head slowly from side to side. No pressure. No pain. He gave a sigh of contentment. At this very moment he was quite glad to be alive.

Wendy brought her dinner into Jamie's room and although they ate in silence, Jamie felt that silence to be companionable.

When they'd finished eating, Wendy took their plates, put them on the floor and said she'd like to talk to Jamie. Would he mind if she turned out the main light and just had the little reading light on? She'd put the reading light over there, on top of the chest of drawers, if he didn't mind. It would be easier for her to talk in the semi-darkness.

'You're so courageous, James, so brave and strong and because of that you may not understand me but I have to tell someone about myself and I've decided that it's you I want to tell. You see, I'm not strong. I'm weak. I sometimes think I'm the weakest person in the world.' Wendy was sitting beside him on the bed but she was not touching him. They were both in the shadows and he could not make out the features of her face. However, he could see her lips moving and he watched them as she spoke. Her hands rested quietly in her lap.

'I was only sixteen when I began university. A child, really. Totally naive and innocent. I'd led a very sheltered life. My parents were both schoolteachers. When they realised how bright I was they encouraged me to accelerate my studies. They didn't think it mattered that when I entered university I was younger than anyone else. They thought it might be best for me to immerse myself totally in the academic world so they arranged for me to live in at a university college. They didn't prepare me in any way for the real world.

'On my first day I attended an introductory lecture given by the Professor of English Language. It's difficult for me to explain to you, James, what happened on that day but the truth is that I looked at the man standing there at the podium, his flowing black robe, his handsome face, his air of intellectual mastery and he seemed to me to take on the dimensions of a god. I fell in love that day, absolutely, completely, unreservedly in love. I knew nothing of love. Yet love took hold of me and I became the victim of an obsession so powerful, so overwhelming, that it virtually took over my life.

'I realise now that my initial response to my Language Professor was a schoolgirl crush, one that I might have been able to get over quite naturally in time but I've never been able to free myself from it. You see, almost immediately, my work began to be noticed and I was singled out for particular attention. I was summoned to the Professor's room. I was told of my promising future. And when I entered his office, alone, sixteen, my adoration for him barely concealed, I evoked a response in him that sparked a passion that neither of us could control. Of course he can't be forgiven for taking advantage of me, for seducing a girl so young and vulnerable and yet I know that my desire matched his and I'm at least partially responsible for the beginning of our affair. For the last five years we have grasped swift, frantic moments of lovemaking. Always in his office. On the floor. On the desk. In the chair. Stolen, secret moments.

'You see, he's forty-three years old. Married. Three small children. He won't destroy his family for me. It's a hopeless love I'm trapped in. It can only result in unhappiness. We both try to stop but somehow the urge is irresistible. I devote myself slavishly to my work but I live for moments of passion I share with him. I have to give him up and yet I can't.

'I've been thinking, James, that you might be able to help me set myself free of him. I was a virgin, of course, when I met him. I've never slept with anyone else. But I've had it in mind, for quite some time, that if I could make myself have an affair with someone else, then perhaps I could break the cycle of need for him. Until this moment, James, I've never told anyone what I'm telling you. It seems to me that you're a very special person because of your suffering. You have sensitivity and inner strength. You might be the right person to help me. You see, I'm weak and I need your strength. And you're so alone. Perhaps you need something from me.'

Jamie was so taken aback that for a moment he could not respond. Of course he would accept Wendy, accept her on any terms at all but she took his silence for reluctance.

'If you don't want to help me, I'd understand. I really would. I'm very grateful that you've listened to me. I can't tell you how relieved I am just to have been able to unburden myself to someone. I feel cleansed by having poured everything out of myself and into you. I'm sure that I could soothe your physical pain and you could soothe my mental anguish. We could help each other, don't you think?'

'Of course we could,' said Jamie and he reached over and took her hand.

'But not for the next few days. I know you mustn't exert yourself. There's plenty of time,' said Wendy. 'All the time in the world.'

When they began making love to each other, Jamie's gratitude was boundless. To be permitted to touch another human being after such a long period of deprivation was an exquisite relief. He adored Wendy and she allowed his adoration. She granted him the right to explore and worship every part of her body and he was so hungry for love that it was very easy for her to satisfy his physical desire. The aim of the exercise, however, was to help Wendy forget her lover and, in this respect, Jamie could only feel that he was failing.

She made love with her eyes closed. Why did she close her eyes? Was she trying to block out the image of her lover's body or was she trying to conjure him up? Or did she close her eyes because the sight of Jamie's misshapen body was so distasteful that she could only make love to him when she couldn't see him? These questions tortured him but he could not give voice to them. She did gain sexual satisfaction but only after hours of gentle foreplay and only by means of slow, careful stimulation of her clitoris with either his tongue or his hand. And often, during those hours, she exhibited a level of frustration that Jamie found disturbing. She would seem to be close to orgasm but then desire would recede and she would thrash around on the bed, trying to recover a level of desire intense enough to reach orgasm. At such times she seemed to be angry with herself and when orgasm finally occurred she would weep with relief and hug Jamie and tell him that he'd done very well, very well indeed. However, he was not reassured. Where were the moments of electric, blinding passion that she had described when recounting the relationship with her English Professor? If she could feel that passion for him then why couldn't she feel it for Jamie? He certainly felt it for her. Indeed, she always insisted that his demanding need for her should be gratified immediately and swiftly before they began the long process of trying to satisfy her. When he entered her, to have his orgasm, she was never in a state of sexual arousal and when she had her orgasm she was always separated from him. She achieved satisfaction only by drifting off into some imagined world of her own. It could have been any tongue, any hand that triggered the final moment of release. So the hours of lovemaking were tinged with sadness and disappointment. Nevertheless, he lived each day for the time he spent with her and wanted nothing more than to be allowed to go on worshipping her body forever.

Three months after he had begun to make love to her she told him that it was no good. It hadn't worked. She was as obsessed as ever with her lover. She'd tried, really tried this time to give him up but she'd failed. She was weak, weak, weak!

'What about me?' Jamie cried. 'What about me?' Didn't he have a right to speak of the anguish and despair that her withdrawal would cause him? Damn her! She was going to leave him to drown in his own loneliness. She'd picked him up, used him and now she was going to throw him away. He was so furious that he kept on shouting, 'What about me? What about me?'

'I'm sorry, James,' she murmured. 'I'm so very sorry.'

Wendy retreated. She avoided Jamie by staying in her room, using the kitchen and bathroom only when absolutely necessary. A week later she told Jessica that she was leaving. She'd found somewhere else to live. She left without speaking to Jamie. Nothing she could have said would have consoled him. His anger with her had given way to anger with himself. What a fool he was! To have hoped, even for one moment, that Wendy might grow to love his crippled body. Loneliness, isolation, alienation - that was all the future had in store for him.

Jamie allowed himself to wallow in self-pity until Wendy moved out but then he pulled himself together. It was getting close to the end of the college year and there was a great deal of work to be done. The loss of Wendy was painful but he was surprised to find that it did not plunge him into deep depression. He needed to develop a philosophy of love that would fit comfortably with a realistic view of his own physical condition. He could not expect to find a love that would last forever. He must be grateful for transitory moments of love. He must cling to the hope that there would be other nights shared with other women. And whenever he was permitted a moment of love he must make the most of it, grab hold of it, enjoy it, hold onto it for as long as he possibly could.

Within a few weeks Avril and Daniel moved in and when they came to stay they brought love of a very different kind. Avril was Michael's twenty-seven-year-old sister and Daniel was her four-year-old son. Jessica had, at first, been reluctant to have a child in the house but it was a difficult time of year to find a new occupant for the room vacated by Wendy and when Michael said that his sister was looking for somewhere to live, Jessica agreed to have them on a trial basis. They could stay for three months. If it didn't work out they'd have to leave.

There was a strong family resemblance. Like Michael, Avril was tall and willowy. Her long, lank, blonde hair almost reached her waist and she did nothing to keep it out of her way but allowed it to fall across her face, often obscuring her features entirely. She wore strange, Kaftan-style dresses which she obviously made herself. They were roughly sewn, made of coarse hemp-like cotton. She wore only solid, subdued colours - brown, tan, beige and olive green. She wore no adornments of any kind. She dressed Daniel in similar, sack-like fashion, in baggy, knee length pants and Kaftan-style shirts. Daniel's shirt always matched the dress his mother had chosen to wear that day and his hair had been allowed to grow to shoulder length. A rough fringe across his forehead prevented his hair from falling into his eyes. They both wore leather sandals.

Daniel was quiet and obedient and it did not take long for Jamie to realise that the child was content because he was adored. Avril was devoted to her son, catering to his every whim, anticipating his needs and desires, devising means to please and amuse him. Avril believed in love. She did not only believe in loving her son. She believed in the existence of a universal power of love that encompassed the world, bestowing its benevolence on every creature that inhabited the globe.

She did not seek to impose her view of the world on others but the way she conducted herself in the house made it impossible to ignore her beliefs. She did not confine herself and Daniel to their room but used the whole house as if it were her own. She baked bread and cooked large quantities of vegetables, inviting anyone who was in the house to join her and Daniel at meal times. Late each afternoon she would have a bath with Daniel. She left the bathroom door open as if it were natural and shameless for a mother and her son to be seen playing naked in the bathtub together.

Avril survived on a single parent's benefit and because she neither worked nor studied she had more time at her disposal than anyone else who lived in the house. She began to take over more than her share of household chores and often baked a cake, which she left on the kitchen table for anyone to help themselves to a slice. Jamie might come home from college to find his bedclothes neatly straightened and a single flower in a small glass of water beside his bed. He assumed that other members of the household found similar evidence of her personal, caring touch. There was no favouritism. Apart from her son, who obviously received special attention, it was clear that Avril put into practice a policy of loving all her fellow human beings equally.

Her philosophy intrigued Jamie and he questioned her about it. He would have given a great deal to be able to share her views. 'If we all allowed ourselves to tap into the universal power of love then the world would be a beautiful place,' said Avril. 'There'd be no hate, only love. No war, only peace. No anger, only harmony. No sorrow, only joy. If we allowed our love to be general, rather than particular, then we'd be much happier. If a man loved all women, instead of one woman; if a woman loved all men, instead of one man, then all the petty troubles that we allow to consume us in our daily lives would disappear. That's how I live my life. If I can live that way, James, so can you.'

But, of course, he couldn't. Nothing in his own experience confirmed the existence of any benevolent force in the universe. If anything, his illness and pain seemed to point instead to the possible presence of something quite cruel and malevolent. At the very best Jamie saw the universe as indifferent to his suffering. Nevertheless, he sought Avril's company and felt himself blessed to be the recipient of her generalised love for all mankind.

The comforting aspect of Avril's kind of loving was that it did not discriminate. Jamie could feel quite certain that, in Avril's eyes, his physical disabilities did not deny him an equal right to be loved. She was just as willing to spend time with him as with anyone else. There was, however, the understood proviso that her kindness and compassion could only be given at moments when Daniel did not need her. So there was a distracted quality to her attention. She was constantly watching the child, listening, anticipating, ready to drop whatever she was doing the moment she sensed his need for her.

When the college year ended, Jamie had two months of free time stretching out in front of him. Jessica, Sean and Michael, who worked part-time throughout the year to support themselves, worked full-time during the long Christmas holidays. Jamie would never have been able to take on the kind of work they did - bar-tending, waiting on tables, washing dishes. He could only cope with the physical demands of the pottery course by spending weekends and holiday periods recovering his strength. He had intended to return to his mother's house and, perhaps, go away on holidays with her, as he had done the previous year, but he felt reasonably well and the company of Avril and Daniel was more attractive to him than the company of his mother.

So he spent the holidays taking Avril and Daniel on outings to the beach, to the mountains, to the north coast, to the south coast. Avril loved nothing better than to play with her son in a natural environment, teaching him to respect and appreciate the wonders of nature. For Jamie, the days were largely spent in watching because, on the whole, he was unable to participate. He was able to swim if they visited a lake or a river but could not risk being knocked over and damaged by the surf. He could walk for a short time on a flat bush track but could not negotiate steep inclines or descents and rough, rocky terrain was out of the question. So he sat and watched or sat and waited, while Avril and Daniel went off to do as they pleased. The constant reminder of his limitations saddened him but his sorrow was never more than mild melancholy. He contemplated nature; he contemplated Avril and Daniel and, on the whole, the days passed calmly and peacefully.

'It's so good of you, James,' she said, 'to take us out.' She was sitting in the car next to him and she touched his arm as she spoke. 'It's wonderful to get out of the city. Sometimes I think I should take Daniel to live in the countryside. What a difference it's made to us, going out like this day after day.'

'Don't go away,' said Jamie.

'Why not,' asked Avril.

'Because I'd miss you,' said Jamie. 'I like to be with you, with you and Daniel. We get along well together, don't we?'

'I get on well with everyone,' said Avril. 'Do you know what would be terrific, James? What if we bought some second hand camping gear. We could get a tent and a few sleeping bags. Then we could stay out and sleep in the bush. What do you think?'

Jamie was willing to do anything that would bring him closer to Avril and he readily agreed. The process of camping, however, proved very painful for him. It was excruciating to lie in a sleeping bag on the ground but the closeness of the other two, curled up next to him in their tiny tent, more than compensated for his agony. He would lie awake, watching them sleep. During these precious hours of the night they looked defenceless and vulnerable; he felt they required his protection. He was beginning to think of Avril as a woman who needed him. She was alone in the world, with a child to rear. Surely she would be better off with the support and love of a man who would gladly devote himself to her and to her son.

As the weeks passed, Jamie became more and more convinced that looking after Avril and Daniel was not only his right but also his destiny. He did not, however, intend to bring up the subject of a future together. Her behaviour towards him made it imperative for him to move slowly. He would do all he could to ingratiate himself with Avril and Daniel until, without their realising it, he had become indispensable to them. When Avril understood that she could not do without Jamie, she would surely agree to marry him and allow him to take on the role of father to Daniel. How wrong he'd been to think he would have to settle for brief moments of love. Here was a ready-made family, needing him to make it complete.

After all the time he had spent with them during the holidays, Jamie did expect to be singled out for particular attention when the household settled down again into its normal routine. It was the third and last year of the pottery course and Jamie needed to work hard at perfecting the techniques he had been taught over the last two years. Pain and exhaustion made camping trips impossible for him but he did try to take Avril and Daniel out into the countryside one day each weekend. Although she always thanked him, she maintained her attitude of loving all the others equally and her failure to see Jamie's special and particular qualities began to irritate him. The months passed by without any change in Avril's behaviour and without any admission on her part that she needed someone like Jamie to take care of her.

It was not difficult to see flaws in Avril's view of life and Jamie began to attack her, trying to break down her defences.

'Do you know what I think, Avril?' he said. 'I think that you're afraid of commitment, afraid of love. You must have been terribly hurt once and you've taken on this pose of loving everyone to protect yourself from ever being hurt again.'

Avril simply smiled, in a self-contained, enigmatic way, obviously unwilling to enter a discussion of such a personal nature. That was the trouble with Avril. She insisted on maintaining calm and equanimity. She was expert at avoiding confrontation. Jamie, however, persisted.

'What about Daniel's father? You never speak of him. Did he hurt you? Damage you? Leave you in the lurch when you needed him?' asked Jamie.

'Not at all,' said Avril. 'He was a quiet, gentle man. I met him up North, when I was passing through. He lived in an old converted dairy in the rain forest area. I wanted a child but I wanted that child to be my own. I never even told him that I was pregnant.'

'But you don't have affairs with men now. That's unhealthy, don't you think? It's abnormal,' said Jamie.

'I have Daniel. Daniel is all I need,' said Avril.

'I admire the way you devote yourself to Daniel,' said Jamie, 'but sometimes I think you're just a puppet to his pleasure.'

'I live my beliefs through Daniel,' she said.

'But don't you think it's bad for him, to always have his needs met? To never know frustration or anger or grief? Don't you think that's unnatural, Avril?'

'I'm not going to argue with you, James.'

'You're not equipping Daniel for the real world. How is he going to cope when he goes to school, when he leaves your full-time care and has to face the truth that you can't have whatever you want in life? I'm not trying to argue with you, Avril. I'm trying to guide you, to help you.'

'I know you mean well, James. And I do love you for your concern,' said Avril.

'When the household breaks up at the end of the year, what are you going to do? What's going to happen to you and Daniel? You need someone to look after you. I can see that so clearly. I don't know why you can't see it yourself,' said Jamie.

'Daniel and I have managed perfectly well so far,' said Avril.

Although Jamie fell short of telling her that he was the right person to look after her, he hoped his message had got through to her. As the year progressed, he continued to believe that she would allow the tight circle of love that bound her to Daniel to be loosened and expanded to include himself.

It was a visit to Luna Park, with Avril and Daniel, that made Jamie realise he was deluding himself. There was a merry-go-round in the park with wooden horses that rose and fell and fixed, swan-shaped carriages designed to seat several people. Daniel, always unwilling to be separated from his mother, at first insisted that she sit beside him in one of the fixed carriages but as he watched the merry-go-round turning and saw other children going up and down on the magical horses, he grew courageous and said he wanted to ride a horse alone. His mother was not to go on the merry-go-round at all but must stand and watch him as he went around. Avril placed Daniel on a smart, black horse, reassured him and then came to stand beside Jamie.

Jamie watched Avril as she watched her son. Her anxious eyes never left him and the child's anxiety was equally obvious. He strained to pick her out in the waiting crowd and each time he caught a glimpse of her his relief was evident. Despite his apprehension, Daniel knew, with unshakeable certainty, that his mother would be there to gather him in her arms when the ride ended and Jamie, witnessing the impenetrable bond that tied the mother to her child felt, in that instant, that he could never be included. They were self-sufficient. They needed no one but each other. When the ride was over Jamie said that he'd like to have a go himself, just for old time's sake. He got onto the horse that Daniel had ridden and as he went around, feeling slightly foolish, he looked for Avril and Daniel in the sea of faces. He thought he saw them but when he got off the merry-go-round at the end of the ride they were nowhere in sight. They hadn't bothered to wait for him. They'd gone off to buy fairy floss at a stall quite a distance away. It took Jamie at least ten minutes to find them.

There was a great deal of discussion in the house about what they would all do at the end of the year. Jessica was going to move to the Blue Mountains. A craft community lived and worked in Leura and she was hoping to find a niche for herself among the artists there. Sean and Michael had located an ideal place for a communal pottery studio. There was a large, derelict warehouse, owned by St Alban's church in Ultimo. They could rent it for next to nothing if they could raise the money to make repairs, put in electrical wiring and plumbing, and fit out the studio with benches, wheels and a kiln. Thousands of dollars would be needed and they were hoping that Jamie would be able to persuade his father to finance their joint enterprise. When Avril said that she'd decided to take Daniel up to the north coast to live, no one was surprised. Jamie had, by now, fully accepted the fact that he would never have a place in their lives.

CHAPTER 4

Walter was adamant. He would not finance the studio. Why should he? He didn't mind spending money but he wasn't going to throw it away. And he certainly wasn't going to put thousands of dollars into helping two other young men who meant nothing to him at all. He knew what his own responsibilities were and he had adequate means to meet those responsibilities but he wasn't going to take on responsibility for people he didn't know. A cooperative pottery studio! He'd never heard of anything so ridiculous in all his life. If Jamie had chosen to spend the last three years amusing himself by doing some meaningless arty-crafty course then that was fine but he didn't really think he could sell those pots, did he? No one in their right mind would buy them.

Jamie was devastated. Walter had struck at the core of his fragile sense of self worth and had shown, yet again, that he had no understanding of Jamie's needs and aspirations. Of course Jamie had doubts, severe doubts about the quality of his own pottery and about the chances of the cooperative succeeding but he was determined to find a way to make a go of it. And Sean and Michael were relying on Walter's help. Jamie had virtually promised his father's financial backing. How was he going to explain to them that his father now refused to support them?

His first reaction to his father's rejection was to turn to his mother for help. 'What about the house, Mum? You own the house outright, don't you? Couldn't we sell the house and divide the money between us? You could buy a comfortable unit. You don't need a house this size and I could use my half of the money to finance the cooperative. There'd be enough for me to buy a small, studio apartment to live in. Please, Mum, I want this so badly.'

'I'm sorry, James. I can't sell the house. It's not for my own sake that I feel the need to hold onto it, but for yours,' said Elizabeth.

'But I need the money and I need it now,' said Jamie.

'I have to think beyond now, James. I have to think of your illness and of the very real possibility that your disease could cause such deterioration in your physical condition that you'll need to be looked after. When and if that happens I intend being the person to look after you and we'd need a house this size.'

'I don't want to be thinking always of disease and death,' he cried. 'I want to live. I want to make something meaningful out of my life. I want this pottery studio. I want it desperately, now, this minute. I don't care if I die by the time I'm thirty if I can just have this chance to make the cooperative work.'

'I'm sorry, James. I really am, but I can't sell the house,' said Elizabeth.

Jamie was furious. Why wouldn't they help him? They were letting him down, both of them, at the time when he most needed their support and understanding. He would have to go back to his father. Walter was the one with the real power. And he wasn't going to beg and plead. He was going to argue and attack. He was going to play on Walter's weaknesses, evoke his father's feelings of guilt and responsibility. He had to get his father to change his mind.

'What about those bonds and shares you've been buying in my name over the years, Dad? They must be worth something now. If they're in my name why can't I cash some of them in so that I can have the money to invest in the cooperative?'

'They're in a trust fund, Jamie. I've set up the fund so that neither you nor I can touch the investments there. If you outlive me then, after my death, the trustees will continue to administer the fund and finance all your living expenses,' said Walter.

'You mean you wouldn't trust me to manage my own finances, even if you lived to be eighty! Do you know how old I'd be then, Dad? I'd be fifty-five years old.'

'As long as I'm alive it's my responsibility to look after you,' said Walter.

'Dad, could you, just for a moment, stop seeing me as your poor crippled boy? I'll be twenty-seven in January. I'm a man, not a boy. And if I have a crippled body that doesn't necessarily mean that I have a crippled mind. It doesn't mean I'm incapable of making decisions about my own future.'

'I don't want to talk about things like this, Jamie. I do my best for you,' said Walter.

'You do what you think is best for me without ever consulting me, without ever considering what I think is best for me. Can't you see that, Dad? Can't you see that I'm not the person you think I am? I'm the person I think I am. Can't you try, Dad, to make an effort to see me as I see myself?'

'You've always had somewhere nice to live, enough to eat, good clothes, a car to drive, plenty of pocket money,' said Walter. 'If you ever decided to marry, I'd buy you a house, pay you an allowance, support your family. You know I would.'

'Then why, why won't you give me the money to get the pottery cooperative going when I'm telling you that this is the thing I want most in the world?'

'It's those other boys. I'm worried about you going into partnership with people who are strangers to me. How do you know you can trust them?'

'Is that your only objection?' Jamie asked.

'That, and the other thing - I don't believe in what you're doing. I don't want to put my money into something that I see as a total waste of time,' said Walter. 'If it were a promising commercial enterprise then I'd be only too happy to finance you but, quite frankly, I think your venture is doomed to failure.'

'Look at you,' said Jamie. 'You're fifty-two years old and you've got so much money that you haven't had to work for the last two years. You pay a manager to run the coffee lounges for you; you've invested in shares and properties; you play golf whenever you please; you go skiing for weeks at a time during the winter; you own a beach house on the south coast and you take your wife and daughter on at least one extended overseas trip a year.'

'I'll tell you what,' said Walter. 'I want you boys to do something to show you're seriously committed to this project of yours. I want the three of you to find a way to raise some of the money yourselves. Let's say I'll give you six months. If you've managed to get a reasonable amount of money together by the end of six months, I'll provide the rest of the finance.'

When Jamie presented Walter's proposition to Sean and Michael they were initially disappointed but immediately set about devising ways and means of meeting Walter's requirements. Everyone who had completed the pottery course had a good deal of work they'd like to sell, so the three of them decided to set up a retail outlet for these ceramics and for the work of any other interested potters. They found a shop to rent in an inexpensive part of Manly. Jamie was to manage the shop, while Sean and Michael took any jobs they could find. St Alban's Church had no one else interested in their derelict warehouse and, for a small down payment, were prepared to allow six months to elapse before signing a two-year lease to rent the area to them as a studio. For the sake of economy, Jamie moved back home with Elizabeth and had cause to be grateful for her help. There were days when he was not well enough to be at the shop alone and, on those occasions, his mother helped him. She enjoyed herself so much that she came regularly to work with him and the business did better for her presence. As a saleswoman she proved to be unobtrusive yet gently persuasive. In the six months the shop showed a small profit and the work undertaken by Sean and Michael provided a few thousand dollars. Walter agreed to fulfil his promise.

It cost much more to fit out the warehouse than anyone had anticipated. It was the basic repairs that proved so costly. Window and doorframes were warped and rotten. An entirely new electrical wiring system had to be installed. The roof leaked and quotes for restoring it were astronomical. Walter would not simply hand over money. He scrutinised every account and insisted that three quotes be obtained for every step of the work. Jamie spent his days chasing up tradesmen, coordinating their work and making sure that his vision for the cooperative was achieved as quickly and as economically as possible. He had never felt so well. His body seemed light and buoyant. He was almost free of pain. If he could have one year like this, just one year of good health, even if that proved to be all the time he had left to live, he'd die happily, willingly.

At last the studio was ready and Jamie could begin to live out the fulfilment of his dream. This was, however, a shared dream and differences of opinion as to how the cooperative should be run were bound to arise. Initially the differences were minor, and for many months Jamie worked happily in what he felt to be a friendly, harmonious environment. The three of them had signed the lease and were jointly responsible for the cooperative. The warehouse was huge and there was room for several potters to work there. Others joined the cooperative by paying a small rent for their space in the studio and use of the equipment. They also paid commission on work sold at the shop, which had been set up at the front of the studio.

Enthusiasm carried them along for the first six months. They knew it would take time for the cooperative to become an economically viable concern and they were prepared to put in maximum effort for little return. Sean and Michael began to voice their discontent when the earnings from the studio continued to provide little more than pocket money. They still had to work at night in dissatisfying, mundane jobs in order to survive. Jamie's attitude was different. All three of them were living the lives of working artists, weren't they? There they were, Monday to Friday, from nine to five, sitting at their wheels, firing the kiln, decorating their vases and plates and bowls. In time their studio would be so well established that the public would flock there to buy the finished products.

'That's alright for you,' said Sean. 'Your father's rich. You'll never have to worry about having enough money for rent and food.'

'If it weren't for my father,' said Jamie, ' you wouldn't have a studio to work in at all.'

'We need to attract some really good potters to work here,' said Michael. 'That's the only way we're going to establish ourselves. We're only getting half-baked amateurs, hopeless people like Helen.'

'There's nothing wrong with Helen,' said Jamie. 'She lacks confidence, that's all. She just needs encouragement.'

'And your idea of opening the studio up to Ultimo kids on Saturday mornings is stupid,' said Sean. 'I mean, what do we get out of that? Teaching kids for nothing.'

'But we agreed, when we set up the studio, that we should try to be part of the community,' said Jamie. 'Those kids are deprived. They come from poor families. They know nothing about art. We're really making a contribution to society by teaching them.'

'We can't afford to work for nothing,' Sean continued. 'I'm not going to do it any more.'

'Don't then,' said Jamie. 'Be selfish. Live just for yourself. I'll look after the kids on my own. I don't need you. I don't need either of you.'

It was true that, so far, the potters who had joined them were mediocre and tended to leave after only a short period of time because the promise of selling their work failed to eventuate. But Jamie was hopeful that this situation would change and he refused to see his own personal participation in the project as a failure. He was doing exactly what he wanted to do and although he had not made much money from the sale of his pottery, he sold two or three pieces of work each week. For the moment, that was enough to satisfy him.

He was upset by Michael's criticism of Helen because he very much wanted Helen to stay at the studio. He knew that her work was not good but she was eager to improve and she looked upon Jamie as someone who could help her to achieve that aim. She admired his work and, he thought, she admired him. He revelled in this attention and he allowed himself to hope that Helen might prove to be the life companion that he had been waiting for. He told himself that, until now, he had been neither physically well enough, nor mentally mature enough, to entertain the possibility of an everlasting love relationship. But now he was well and here was Helen.

They ate lunch together each day. She was, Jamie thought, open and honest with him. She confided in him her fear of failure. 'I've tried so many things, James. And I seem to have failed at all of them. When I left school I was determined to become an actress. I stuck it out for five years, going to drama classes, getting small parts in amateur productions. When I realised I wasn't going to make it, that I just wasn't good enough, I had a kind of breakdown. I couldn't make myself get out of bed. I stayed there for five months. I had to have help - medication, therapy - that sort of thing. And then I thought I'd try painting. I was always drawing when I was a kid. I'm very good at it. Very accurate and life-like. But the same thing happened. I just wasn't good enough to be special. And now I'm doing pottery. I have to succeed this time. What do you think, James? Will I ever be any good?'

'Of course you will,' said Jamie and he really wished that what he was saying would turn out to be the truth. He could not bear to see her so sad. His heart went out to her and he felt her sadness as if it were his own. He wanted to free her from her sorrow by loving her. Surely love could save her. If he made a commitment to her, promised to love her for all eternity, perhaps she would reciprocate by loving him. They could find together a love that would enrich both their lives and banish sorrow forever.

He would, however, move cautiously. The way for him to win Helen was to make it clear to her that he had something that she needed. She thought that what she needed was to succeed at her pottery but he could see that she was really searching for love. He would help her as much as he possibly could in the studio and he would watch and wait. She might improve. On the other hand, the time might come when she realised that she wasn't going to achieve her goal and, if that happened, he wanted to be there at the moment when she acknowledged her failure as a potter. He wanted to catch her when she fell. And then he would offer her himself, his true and honest heart, his empathy, his love. Surely she would understand that what he had to give was worthy of acceptance.

Although Helen was aware that Sean and Michael thought very little of her work, it was Jamie she believed, partly because she wanted to believe him and partly because he seemed to have more authority than anyone else in the studio. He behaved, always, as if he were in charge. It was this attitude that rankled and irritated Sean and Michael to the point of outright rebellion.

'You have to stop carrying on as if you own this place,' said Sean. 'It's not your studio. It's ours. A cooperative. No one has any more authority than anyone else. We're not going to put up with it much longer.'

'And what are you going to do about it?' asked Jamie. 'My name's on the lease. My father supplied the money.'

'That was almost a year ago. How long do you expect us to go on being grateful to you?' said Michael.

'If I didn't take control, this place would fall apart,' said Jamie. 'Look what happened last week with the kiln. I packed it, put it on and you two were supposed to turn it off. You left it on too long, didn't you? All the glazes were burnt. The whole lot ruined. All my work, all Helen's work and the pots the kids made at the Saturday workshop. You can't be trusted. And do you really think you'd clean up your mess if I didn't nag at you? This place would look like a pigsty if I didn't keep charge.'

'We're warning you, James,' said Michael. 'We've had enough. Either you change your attitude or we'll find some way to get rid of you.'

'You can't get rid of me,' said Jamie. 'My name's on the lease.'

The atmosphere soured. Conspiracies and divisions arose. People whispered in corners but Jamie did nothing to moderate his behaviour. Jamie seemed to have forgotten that the cooperative was originally Sean and Michael's idea. He had turned it into the fulfilment of his own personal dream and he could not permit anyone to undermine him. He was convinced that the day to day functioning of the studio would be impossible without his management. However, he began to see that perhaps the very idea of a cooperative was unworkable. He might need to use the studio as a stepping stone. He should aim at having a place of his own, where his authority would never be questioned. He would assess the situation at the end of the two-year lease. Meanwhile he would continue to exercise control. There was nothing anyone could do about it. The tension, however, was unpleasant and when Jamie looked around at the others who were sharing the studio, he realised that he did not know how many of them supported him. The only person he could rely on was Helen.

He continued to court her, to encourage her, to praise her work. He also invited her, as a friend, to join him in a meal at a restaurant, to go with him to a film, to have dinner at his mother's house, to enjoy a swim in his father's pool. She accepted his invitations and behaved in an easy, friendly manner. She always thanked him for his attention in the studio and expressed her appreciation whenever she went out with him but gave no indication that she saw their association as anything more than a platonic friendship. She did not kiss his cheek when she said goodnight, nor did she put out her hand to take his arm as they walked down the street. All that, however, would change in time. Jamie was quite sure of it.

If Helen had not been such a staunch ally in the studio, then Jamie might have felt more threatened by the disloyalty of Sean and Michael. He was, however, so used to ostracism and alienation that he regarded their defection as simply another example of unfair rejection. He could not see that his own behaviour had contributed to the rift between them. People were intolerant. It had been that way since he'd first contracted this wretched illness. Never mind. He had Helen's support and her loyalty gave him a false sense of security. But then a new potter came to work at the studio. His name was Mark, and his arrival would change the dynamics of the cooperative and force Jamie to realise that his position was truly in danger.

Mark was older than anyone else working in the studio. He had been a high school art teacher for twelve years. When he applied to join the cooperative he explained that he was taking a year off to find out whether he could succeed as a potter. If, after twelve months of full-time effort, he could not make a living from his art then he would accept the necessity of returning to teaching.

'All art teachers are frustrated artists, you know. We'd all prefer to live by our art than to teach it. I'm single; I don't have any family to support. I'll be thirty-five this year. If I don't give it a go now, it might be too late. The set-up you've got here is ideal for my purposes. I hope you won't feel I'm too old to join you.'

Jamie assured Mark that the cooperative did not practice discrimination and that, in any case, he was only six or seven years older than they were themselves. Sean and Michael agreed that Mark would make a welcome addition to the studio. He quickly moved in and began his work. He was a quiet, unassuming man of medium height and slight build whose only visible eccentricity was shoulder length hair which he wore in a tight, neat plait while he was working. His clothes were always fresh and clean and he covered them by wearing a long, loose, khaki smock in the studio.

He became, almost immediately, a calming influence in the cooperative because he took no notice of the tensions and divisions that seemed to preoccupy the other members. When there were arguments or differences of opinion, he took no part in them and behaved as if they weren't happening. This attitude had the effect of reinforcing his maturity and making the others, by comparison, appear petty and infantile. They began to think twice before bickering with each other and less time was devoted to huddled whispering behind people's backs. Mark worked from morning till night, never stopping, never speaking unless spoken to and his example was a reminder of what they were all there for.

Within two weeks they realised he was a genius. His designs were outrageous, bold and bizarre. The irregular shapes of his bowls, his cups, his vases seemed to defy all the rules and yet they were spectacular. The colours and patterns he chose to decorate his work were unique and daring. Everyone in the studio gazed with awe at the range and originality of the work he had produced by the end of a month.

His work began to sell. By the end of the second month everything he produced was regularly being sold. By the end of the third month people were putting in orders for sets of plates and dishes, coffee pots, salt and pepper shakers, salad bowls. He could not produce as much as he was able to sell. More and more buyers came to the cooperative and this benefited all the members. Not every buyer wanted to purchase Mark's pottery. Many people preferred more conventional designs and there was a steady increase in sales. The cooperative was, at last, doing what it had been set up to do. It was providing its members with a moderate, steadily growing income.

Jamie should have been delighted with this change of fortune but, in fact, he was ambivalent about the growing success of the cooperative. He struggled to maintain control only to be confronted by other people making decisions without consulting him. He had always been the one to decide when the kiln would be fired but one day, when he arrived at the studio, he found it operating when he had given no instructions for a firing to take place.

'Who put on the kiln?' he demanded to know.

'I did,' said Mark.

'Why didn't you consult me?' asked Jamie.

'I don't need to consult you. I've got orders to fill and commitments to meet. I'll put the kiln on whenever I think it necessary.'

'You should have asked me,' Jamie insisted. 'It's my kiln. My father paid for it.'

'I pay rent to you for my space in the studio,' said Mark, 'and the cooperative is earning an enormous amount in commission on the sale of my work. I have the right to use the kiln whenever I choose to do so.'

And Jamie had no choice but to turn away and walk out of the studio for a while until his anger and frustration had subsided. It wasn't fair. Why did it have to be Mark's work that made such a difference? Why couldn't his own pottery have been recognised as the work of a genius? He was consumed by bitter jealousy. If only he had normal hands, hands that were not swollen or twisted or deformed. Then he, like Mark, could have produced works of such originality that people would have flocked to buy them. It was so unjust. To be restrained and limited by physical shortcomings.

It was not only Mark who threatened Jamie's authority. Sean and Michael had begun to see that it might be possible to live on their earnings from the cooperative if their living expenses could be curtailed in some way. Without asking Jamie they had moved two small stretcher beds into the studio and they'd begun to sleep there so that they wouldn't have to pay rent.

'But you can't do this,' said Jamie. 'I won't have it.'

'We're doing it,' said Michael. 'It'll only be for a few months. There's nothing you can do about it.'

'It's illegal to live here,' said Jamie. 'I'll report you.'

'You do that, James, and I'll find some way to get rid of you; I swear I will,' said Sean. 'Why are you behaving like this? The cooperative is succeeding at last. Why can't you be joyful about it? And grateful, like the rest of us.'

And Jamie had no answer to give. He could not be joyful because it was no longer his cooperative. Little by little Mark and Sean and Michael were taking it away from him. And the loss was too painful to bear. In his desperation to hold onto what he saw as his rightful place in the studio, he allowed his bitterness to spill over into his lunchtime conversations with Helen. But, somehow, Helen was less supportive than she had been. She was no longer prepared to agree with everything he had to say and sometimes she even avoided him altogether. She spent a considerable amount of her time watching Mark work and often, when he expected her to join him for lunch, he found her in Mark's company. This made him so angry that he confronted her.

'Why are you spending so much time with Mark?' he wanted to know.

'He's a marvellous potter. I hope to learn something from him,' Helen replied.

'But what about me? ' Jamie asked. 'You were quite happy to spend your time with me until he came here.'

'What do you want from me, James?' asked Helen. 'I can't see that I'm doing anything that should offend you,'

'What do I want from you? I thought we had a relationship,' said Jamie. 'I thought we owed each other loyalty.'

'We're friends, James. Just friends who work together. We don't have a relationship,' said Helen.

'But you went out with me, quite regularly I thought, to dinner, to the movies, to visit my parents. I thought you liked me. I thought that you could love me. I hoped that one day you would marry me.' Jamie looked at Helen and he could see that what he'd said had horrified and repelled her.

'But James, I could never love you, not like that!' Even as she spoke Jamie could see what a fool he'd been. Why did he always make the mistake of believing that others could see beyond his crippled body and acknowledge his inner worth?

At this moment it seemed that everyone at the studio was against him but he was not going to be defeated. He would keep working there, even if they forced him into total isolation.

Jamie decided to go to the studio very early the next morning even though he was in pain. His head was spinning and his hands ached so badly that he'd had to take an extra dose of painkillers in order to leave the house. Elizabeth had begged him not to go, to stay in bed and rest. She could judge the amount of pain he was in by the heavy labouring of his breath when he slept. Last night his breathing had been so loud and so uneven that she'd had to lie awake listening for the next breath. It was the drugs he took that made his breathing so ragged and distorted. She knew that his abuse of medication could do him great damage but she couldn't argue about it with him. He had a small suitcase full of drugs and at night he arranged his pills in a saucer beside his bed, ready to be taken whenever he needed them. And he'd been so well, relatively free of pain for so long. He'd told her something of the tensions at the studio but she knew that the situation was worse than he was prepared to admit to. She could only hope that circumstances would improve, hope that Jamie did not do anything further to antagonise those with whom he shared the studio. She was on his side, of course she was, but she knew how difficult and demanding he could be. He did not seem to understand that his anger about his physical disabilities often led him to behave irrationally, that his desperate need for acceptance could so easily alienate others. She'd tried to warn him when he left.

'Don't be so angry,' she'd said. 'You can't think clearly when you're angry.'

'Angry? How can I help being angry?' he'd said, as he slammed the door and left the house. By the time he arrived he had a blinding headache and his temples throbbed with pent-up anger. It was so early that he managed to find a parking spot right outside the studio. He locked his car, walked the few steps to the door and put his key into the lock to let himself in. The key would not turn. The door would not open. At first he thought that the pain in his hands had made his fingers clumsy so he struggled with the key, taking it out, inserting it again, jiggling it around in the lock but all his efforts failed. The key would not open the door. And then he realised what they'd done. They'd changed the lock to keep him out! He was so furious that he banged his fists against the door. He shouted and screamed and cursed. He knew Sean and Michael were in there. They'd put in the stretcher beds. They were sleeping inside. They must be able to hear him. He continued to bang on the door, shouting out their names but they would not let him in.

Alright. If they were going to behave like that then he knew exactly how to retaliate. He drove home at high speed, picked up his copy of the lease, rang an Ultimo locksmith and arranged to meet him at the studio in half an hour's time. He refused to answer his mother's questions about what was wrong but left immediately to drive back to the studio. He was going to be calm. He was going to be controlled. He was going to have justice.

It was still only 8.30 a.m. when the locksmith arrived. Jamie showed him the lease, provided proof of his own identity, explained that others had illegally changed the lock and asked the locksmith to oblige him by putting in a new lock. When the door was opened, Jamie expected to confront Sean and

Michael, cowering inside the studio, but they were not there. They must have been too afraid to face the consequences of their actions. They arrived, with the others, shortly after 9 a.m., as if they had all met one another by pre-arrangement. When they walked in, Jamie was sitting at his wheel, working. He did not look up. He did not acknowledge their presence in any way. He went on tending his clay as if the process were absorbing his entire attention. He would not allow them to see that the pain in his neck and back was so excruciating that he feared he might faint. Two hours later he stopped work and left the studio. He had spoken to no one. No one had spoken to him.

He did not know where to go or what to do. Everything he held dear was threatened. For almost eighteen months he had controlled the studio and now he stood alone, unwanted, unappreciated. The pain spread, permeating every joint and muscle in his body but he could not go home. Going home would be admitting defeat. Elizabeth would question him and he was so suffused with pain that he would weaken, succumb to her queries, confess to the failure of his role in the cooperative. And he mustn't do that. He must find a way to survive this challenge to his place in the studio.

He would, however, have to find somewhere to sit down. He had walked away from the studio with no destination in mind but every step he took was laboured, even though he was using his walking sticks. His breathing was hard and heavy and he had broken into a sweat from the effort of keeping going. He found himself in an unfamiliar street but he could see a small coffee lounge in the next block. He'd make his way there, have a cappuccino and think about what he was going to do. His body gave a shudder of relief as he sat down and ordered his coffee. He took his time drinking it. He found that he could not think so he simply allowed his mind and his eyes to wander. His attention was caught by a small sign on a shabby building across the street. The sign said 'MASSAGE'. That was all. Just one word. What kind of massage? There were brothels throughout the area. Was it a brothel? Or did they offer real massages? His pain and his exhaustion were so great that he was not thinking of sex. However, the possibility of having the tension removed from his body by means of massage was so appealing that he paid for his coffee and made his way across the street.

The interior of the building was more attractive than its exterior. He had to walk up one flight of old wooden stairs but when he rang the bell of the massage parlour he was immediately let into a comfortable furnished reception area. A pleasant looking girl, in a white uniform, had answered the door and welcomed him.

'Good morning,' she said. 'Do you have an appointment?'

'No,' said Jamie. 'No, I don't. I was just sitting in that coffee lounge over there and I saw your sign. If anyone ever needed a massage, it's me, so I thought I'd come over.'

'That's fine,' the girl replied. 'Christine is free. She'll look after you. Do you want a straight massage or do you want hand relief as well?' So it was a brothel, after all. Jamie hesitated and blushed. 'You don't have to decide right now. Just see how you feel. Would you like to have a shower before your massage? Here's a nice, clean towel for you. The bathroom's the second door down on the left. When you've finished just go into the room right opposite the bathroom. Christine will join you there.'

The room Jamie entered after his shower was large and sparsely furnished. A massage table with crisp white sheets took its place at the centre of the room. Close to the table was a small stand holding various kinds of oils and lotions. There was a chair in one corner and a small divan stood against one of the walls. Jamie put his clothes on the chair and got onto the massage table, pulling a sheet up over him. When Christine entered the room she immediately set about putting him at ease. Jamie noted that she was also wearing a white uniform. Her dark hair was straight, neat and shoulder length. She was short and solidly built, looked clean and healthy and would, Jamie thought, be in her mid twenties.

'Hello, James. I'm Christine,' she said, accompanying her words with what appeared to be a genuine smile. 'I'm told that you're in great need of a massage.'

'I certainly am,' said Jamie. 'I ache from head to foot. I hope you can help me.'

'Why don't you roll over onto your stomach and I'll start with your neck and shoulders. I always find that if you can get rid of the tension in the neck first then the whole body relaxes more easily.'

Christine's hands were firm but gentle and Jamie felt that they moved with meaning. When she remarked on how tight his shoulder muscles were, he found himself confiding in her, telling her about his work as a potter, explaining that there were some difficulties, at the moment, in the studio where he worked. She sympathised with him and said she'd like to help him. She hoped the massage would provide him with relief from the troubles that beset him. He should close his eyes, let go of his worries, allow her to work on his aching limbs. Her voice, like her hands, was gentle, soothing, mesmerising and he allowed himself to relax beneath her expert touch. He caught himself thinking that his doctors had failed to ease his pain, even though they'd been paid a great deal of money to do so, whereas this massage parlour girl was achieving instantaneous results.

After working on his neck, shoulders, back and legs for half an hour, it was time for him to turn over and, while he was doing so, Christine took off her uniform and performed the rest of the massage dressed only in a pair of brief panties. While she was massaging, she allowed her breasts to brush against him. She let her hand linger on his penis and it responded with an automatic erection. It seemed the most natural thing in the world for her to take his penis in her hand and bring him gently to orgasm. When she'd finished he felt completely at ease. While Jamie was getting dressed he told himself that such gentle hands could only belong to a person with a gentle soul. It was true that he had paid for Christine's services but she had pleased him so greatly that he wanted to do something to please her. He would go back to the studio and make a pot, especially for her, and he would give it to her the next time he came to visit.

When Jamie returned to the studio he was calm, relaxed and free of pain. How he wished he could tell the others that he'd met a marvellous girl, a girl who was kind and gentle and good, a girl whose hands had magically removed every skerrick of anger and tension from his body. But, of course, he could not say anything. He had paid the girl and that made the experience shameful. And, in any case, those who shared the studio were no longer his colleagues, no longer his friends. They had become the enemy. Although he did not know what to do about the situation at the cooperative, he had decided what he would not do. He would not be dismissed. He would not be kicked out. They could change the locks every day if they wanted to. He would simply have them changed back again. He would turn up at the studio each day. He would do his work. He would wait and see what they did next. For the moment it seemed as if the policy they were following was to ignore him. Before he left for the day, he took the two extra keys that had been provided for the new lock. He put one down in front of Mark and the other in front of Sean. Although they both looked up at him when he put the keys down, neither of them spoke to him.

The pot Jamie was making for Christine was not ready by the time he next felt the need to visit her. The undercurrent of animosity in the studio kept tension at a knife's edge and only one day elapsed before he decided to go back to the massage parlour. He did, however, want to bring Christine a gift so he picked out one of his most attractive small vases to take with him. Jamie's effusiveness clearly embarrassed Christine.

'You helped me so much, Christine, more than I can say. I want you to have this,' said Jamie. 'There's another pot coming. One I'm making especially for you but I'll give it to you next time.'

'I can't accept this, James,' said Christine.

'Please, please take it. You could come to my studio, if you liked. You seemed interested when I told you about the pottery. You could have a go at making a pot yourself. I could show you how to do it.'

'I don't think I'd be much good at that,' said Christine. 'I don't like accepting gifts, James. You pay for my services. That's all that's necessary. If you insist, I'll keep this little vase but you mustn't bring me anything else.' And without further conversation she set about doing what she was paid to do.

That night Jamie wrote a note to Christine and he put it under the door of the massage parlour early the next morning. He needed to explain to Christine exactly how he felt about her.

Dear Christine,

*I can tell that you are a woman of kindness, gentleness
and understanding. I know that I could talk to you about
anything at all. And because I feel so at ease with you, I
brought you a piece of my pottery as a gift of gratitude.
Surely there can be nothing offensive about that. I hope
that we can be friends. If the day ever does come when I
can call you a friend then I know that, from that day on,
love will never end.*

Regards,

James

Two days later, carrying the new pot he'd made, Jamie
turned up at the massage parlour. He had his shower, went
into the massage room and lay down on the table, eagerly
awaiting the moment when Christine would come into the
room. There was a knock on the door and a woman Jamie had
never seen before let herself into the room.

'Where's Christine?' he asked.

'Christine's not available at the moment, James. I'm Katherine. I'll be giving you your massage today.'

'But it's Christine I want,' said James. 'I don't know you.'

'Christine was a stranger to you when you first came here,
less than a week ago. We're all properly trained to do our work
here. I guarantee that within ten minutes you won't be able to
tell the difference.'

'No,' said Jamie, getting up and starting to put on his clothes.
'No, I'll wait. I'll come back another time when Christine is free.'

'I'm sorry, James, but Christine won't be available for you,'
said Katherine.

'What do you mean?'

'I mean that we run a business here, James. We service our clients. We don't become involved with them,' said Katherine.

Jamie was so mortified that his face flushed and his heart began to pound in his chest. He finished dressing as quickly as he could and rushed out of the massage parlour. Down the street he fled, forcing his legs to carry him at a pace that was well beyond his normal capacity. The shame of it! To be discarded, rejected by a prostitute in a massage parlour! How could he ever live with such humiliation! Though the studio offered him no haven he plunged towards it. As he reached the entrance a hot, searing pain began on the left side of his chest. It ran down his left arm and up into his throat, accompanied by a wave of intense nausea. He staggered inside, clutching wildly at his heart and fell to the floor. The other members of the cooperative looked at him in stunned and terrified silence.

Mark was the first to react. He called an ambulance and tried to make Jamie comfortable. Sean and Michael came to his aid.

'James, are you alright?' said Sean. 'James, what's wrong with you?' But Jamie could not reply. His chest felt as if it might explode. He could only take in short, sharp, shallow breaths that made speech quite impossible.

'I think he's had a heart attack,' said Mark.

'Oh God,' said Michael, 'is this our fault?'

'I don't know,' Mark replied.

The ambulance arrived quickly and took Jamie to the casualty department at Royal North Shore hospital. He was attended to immediately and although the pain had subsided he was placed in Intensive Care for twenty-four hours. It was a heart attack and further tests would have to be done to determine the extent of the damage. He was put into a private room in the Cardiac Wing for three days. The attack had been terrifying and, for once, Jamie was grateful to be in hospital. Although they seemed to be subjecting him to every test imaginable, he felt at ease in a room of his own. Elizabeth spent as much time with him as the hospital would allow and Walter called in twice a day for brief visits. The pain in the chest had disappeared quickly but Jamie remained short of breath. This was of great concern to the doctors. They preferred that visitors be kept at a minimum but when Mark turned up, wanting to see Jamie on behalf of all the members of the cooperative, he was allowed in for a few minutes.

'We're very sorry about this, James,' said Mark. 'Sorry that you're ill and sorry if our actions contributed in any way to your heart attack. We didn't want to kill you. We just wanted to ….'

'Kick me out. Get rid of me,' said Jamie.

'Things had reached an impasse. We couldn't go on the way we were going. There had to be a change,' said Mark.

'You mean I had to change,' said Jamie.

'Yes, that's exactly what I mean,' said Mark.

'I knew how the place should be run and I ran it well. You've taken that away from me. I don't think I can change,' said Jamie.

'That's up to you,' said Mark. 'I believe it's going to be six weeks before you'll be able to come back to the studio. You're welcome back if you're prepared to take your place as just one of the cooperative's decision makers.'

'I'll think about it,' said Jamie.

Hospital was a miserable place at the best of times but during those three days in the Cardiac Wing Jamie was given close and careful attention. It was comforting to be fussed over in such a way. The nurse with the pill trolley had a wonderful smile. She would ask him what he needed for pain and her voice was so pleasant that the pain would be eased almost before he popped the white pills into his mouth. It seemed to Jamie that he was surrounded by dedicated people who were doing their best to help him.

And then they moved him. The doctors were more worried about his lungs than his heart and, for this reason, the proper place for him was the Thoracic Unit. He no longer had a room of his own but had to share with three others. The outlook was pleasant. The room had a large verandah overlooking gardens and lawns, which could be seen through the sliding doors. However, the view could not compensate for the horror within the ward. The men he had to share with appeared to Jamie to be nothing more than warmed up corpses. They were old, sickly men who gasped for air and continually coughed up phlegm from congested chests. They made disgusting noises, day and night. Did it take practice to snore and fart at the same time or was this a natural state for putrid, ageing bodies?

On his first night in the ward he found the noise intolerable. He pressed his buzzer and asked the night nurse for more sleeping pills but she refused him. She could only give him the medication he had been prescribed. If he wanted more than this he would have to sort it out with the doctor in the morning. There was nothing she could do. She could not act without the authority of a doctor. Jamie was furious. He cursed her for her inhumanity and demanded to see a doctor, now, right this minute. He made such a fuss that the nurse came back with a sister of higher rank who took pity on him and gave him the pills he'd demanded.

The next morning he was amazed when one of the corpse-like patients spoke to him. 'Do you like my flowers?' the old man asked.

'Yes,' said Jamie, 'they're very nice.' How easy it was to see the beauty in a flower, how painful to witness that old men wither and die. Jamie hoped that he would die before he ever came to look like the three men who shared his room.

When the young registrar made his rounds, shortly after breakfast, Jamie took up the matter of medication with him. Jamie had, after all, been suffering from rheumatoid arthritis for nineteen years. He knew what drugs he needed and he knew what quantities he needed them in. Yes, he was in the Thoracic Unit but his lungs were not his only problem. He could feel the onset of joint pain. The matter needed to be addressed immediately. He could not be left to lie here, helpless, without the medication he was accustomed to taking. The doctor said 'No' to Jamie's plea for more pills. Jamie was distraught.

'Look at you, standing there,' said Jamie. 'You think you're God, don't you! You might be the doctor but I'll tell you something. I know a lot more about my disease than you'll ever know. I know what I need to control the pain.'

'You're taking an adequate amount of analgesics. We're worried about the lesions in your lungs and in your heart. We can't prescribe any stronger medication at this stage. I'm sorry but, for the time being, you'll have to go along with our decision,' said the doctor.

Jamie complained to his mother and asked her to bring in drugs from his supply at home but she couldn't agree to do so. 'Please, James, don't ask me to do anything like that. You know I can't. You'll only be here for a few weeks. You'll have to do what the doctors say.' A few days later Jamie saw an old man die. It happened during the day, with the sun flickering through the silent trees. The old man's breath was harsh, rasping and then, quite suddenly, it ceased altogether. There was no one in attendance in the room at the time. Jamie had to go out and find one of the nurses to tell her that a fellow patient had died.

The doctors and nurses of the Thoracic Unit were relieved when it was time for Jamie to go home because he had been such an angry, obnoxious, uncooperative patient. Walter picked him up to drive him home. He came armed with boxes of chocolates to distribute to the staff but their smiles and thankyous barely concealed the fact that they were glad to see the last of Jamie. He was told to report to the Thoracic Clinic in the hospital's Outpatient's Department in a week's time. The wind was surprisingly sharp for early March and the sky was bleak and grey the morning that he left the hospital.

'How do you feel?' asked Walter, as they got into the car.

'Cold. Tired. Depressed. How would you expect me to feel?' said Jamie.

'Would you like to go down to the beach house with your mother for a few weeks?'

'No, I don't want to go anywhere.'

'I know there was trouble at the studio,' said Walter.

'I don't want to talk about that,' said Jamie.

'I'm sorry you've been hurt. I tried to warn you about trusting others,' said Walter.

'Are you going to say, "I told you so", because I don't want to listen to your platitudes.'

'I only want to help you,' said Walter.

'You can't help me. No one can help me,' said Jamie. 'I wish I'd never been born.'

'You have to make the best of things, Jamie.'

'Another platitude,' said Jamie. 'Can you give me a new body, a new heart, new lungs? You can't give me anything that I need. I wish you'd realise that.'

'You'll feel more positive in a few weeks' time,' said Walter. 'When you've got your strength back.'

'Do you know what, Dad? Sometimes I curse you - you and Mum - because you're the ones responsible for putting me on this earth.'

'I wish you wouldn't talk like that, Jamie. It breaks my heart,' said Walter.

'Then suffer. I don't care,' said Jamie. They had nothing further to say to each other until they arrived home.

As they got out of the car, Walter turned to Jamie. 'I've got a surprise for you, son. Come to the garage with me before I take your things inside. I know you had your birthday a few months ago, but I thought I'd get you another present. I wanted to cheer you up a bit.' When Walter opened the door of the double garage, Jamie could see that his twelve-year-old, red M.G. was no longer there. It had been replaced by a small, sleek, brand new, black Jaguar. Walter was so pleased with himself for thinking of buying Jamie a new car that, if Jamie had been able to look at him, he would have seen a broad grin on his father's face.

'That must have cost you a fortune,' said Jamie, as he walked towards the internal garage door that led into the house. He could not face his father because then Walter would have seen that he was crying.

The first week home, Jamie spent a lot of time in his room. The room felt like a prison but imprisonment suited him at the moment. The grey skies had brought several days of continuous rain and the house was cold and dark. The room became more depressing every day. He'd forgotten how it felt to be alive. He lay on his bed with the door closed. No matter how deathly his small room might be, it seemed infinitely safer than the world outside the room. His body shivered. Although he wore several layers of clothing he could not keep warm. The iciness was death. Death was inevitable. Until recently the knowledge of the inevitability of death had been theoretical but that moment of the heart attack, when he'd had to fight for the breath to stay alive, had brought him face to face with the certainty of his own death. Now the thought of death obsessed him. He was a young man. Only twenty-nine years old. How could he live with the absolute, definite truth that he could die at any time? He'd be lucky if he were still alive on his thirtieth birthday. He wished the earth would collide with a massive meteor from outer space. If he had to be snatched away by early death, then he wanted the whole world, and everyone in it, to be smashed and destroyed - to die with him. There would be more heart attacks. He had been assured of that and the next one, or the one after that, or the one after that would kill him. How did one live with death? And, moreover, how did one live with death when the quality of life was so appalling? He would always be alone. And if he was destined to live the rest of his meagre life without love, was it worth living at all?

He could not even bring himself to try out the new car until the day he was due to present himself at the Outpatients Clinic. He unlocked the car and slid into the comfortable driver's seat. The smell of new, soft leather was almost intoxicating. When he turned on the ignition and felt the power of the engine beneath his touch he could not help but feel a thrill of excitement. The weather had cleared. The sky was blue. The sun was shining. And he had, after all, managed to get himself out of the house.

The Outpatients waiting area was depressing. The faces of the patients were grim, apprehensive, with the occasional smile of nervousness. Cleaners polished the floors, blank expressions of boredom on their faces. Nurses hurried about, clean and tidy, neat and efficient, scarcely noticing the anxiety of those who sat there, awaiting a miracle. Jamie felt quite detached from his fellow patients. He knew that there would be no miracle for him. The doctors in white coats sat behind closed doors, holding court, calling upon their wisdom and their accumulated knowledge, writing notes on patients' cards, saying 'Yes', 'I see' and 'Hmm.' No doubt, at the end of a morning clinic they might congratulate themselves on a job well done. Jamie had lost faith in doctors. They were not going to be able to find a cure for him.

It was impossible for Jamie to free himself from despondency. His old school friend, Judy, did her best to keep him going. 'You can't just give up, James,' she said. 'You don't know how long you've got to live. But then none of us does. I could be run over by a bus tomorrow. You have to conduct your life as if you're going to live forever.'

'That's alright for you. You expect to have a normal lifespan,' said Jamie. 'It's very easy to say that your life might be cut short by an accident but what if you knew for certain that such a thing would happen. How would you feel then?'

'I don't know,' said Judy. 'I'm trying to put myself in your place. I really am. All I can tell you is that if I knew I didn't have a long time to live, I wouldn't be sitting around feeling sorry for myself. I'd try to enjoy the time I had left. I'd keep doing the things I loved doing. And you love working with clay. You find it fulfilling and meaningful. If I were you I'd go on with the pottery and every night, before I went to sleep, I'd tell myself that I was going to be alive tomorrow. The doctors haven't placed any definite time limit on your life. You could live longer than anyone imagines possible. You could have so many tomorrows, James, really you could.'

'It's so depressing to live without love,' Jamie replied.

'I live without love,' said Judy.

When Jamie returned to work at the studio he immediately felt that he did not belong there. During the six weeks that he had been away, Mark had taken control and supervised the day to day operation of the cooperative with quiet authority. Nobody seemed to object to this state of affairs. Jamie worked quietly for the first week, observing the situation before confronting Mark.

'I thought we had a cooperative going here, Mark,' said Jamie. 'It seems to me that you're the one making all the decisions. I haven't been asked for my opinion on anything since I came back.'

'No, well, things have changed a bit while you've been away,' said Mark. 'We've had a letter from St. Alban's Church. They're not going to renew our lease at the end of June. They're going to auction the property. I've been to the bank and arranged finance. I'm going to buy the building at the auction and have it as my personal studio. I suppose you could say I've been preparing for the time when I'll be taking over the place as my own. I know your father put a lot of money into setting up the cooperative. After the auction I want you to feel free to take any of the equipment you need for your own use. Of course, fixtures like the kiln can't be moved but you're welcome to anything else.'

'What about you two?' asked Jamie, turning to Sean and Michael. 'How can you just let Mark take over everything that we've built up?' Neither Sean nor Michael replied. They were both looking down at the floor in embarrassment.

'I've offered them both a place in my studio,' said Mark. 'They're dedicated potters. Their work is selling well. They'll be an asset to my business.'

'So you've offered them a place but there's no place for me. Is that right?' said Jamie.

'I'm sorry, James. Your health is precarious. Your output is small. I'll be borrowing a lot of money. I have to run the place as a viable economic concern.'

'I see,' said Jamie. 'And what makes you so sure you'll be able to buy the property? Someone might outbid you.'

'I don't think there are too many people looking for old warehouses,' said Mark.

'I might buy it,' said Jamie.

'It's an open, public auction, James. If you want to bid against me then you have every right to do so,' said Mark.

Jamie turned away from Mark and left the studio. He ought to be angry but he was so deeply hurt that, for the moment, he was insensible to feeling. The idea of bidding against Mark at the auction was, of course, quite ludicrous. He had no money of his own and even if Walter was prepared to provide the finance, that would not solve the problem. The cooperative was finished. Sean and Michael had abandoned him. Mark had dealt the final blow. No one wanted him. He was of no value to himself or to anyone else. He could not think of a single reason for wanting to stay alive.

He drove home steeped in despair. It was late Friday afternoon and even his mother had abandoned him today. She had a long-standing arrangement to play bridge in Canberra this weekend and she would have left by the time he arrived home. Judy had said she might call over tonight but the arrangement was not definite. Jamie put his car in the garage and let himself into the house. Although it was not yet dark, he went through the rooms, turning on all the lights. He did not want to think about the implications of today. He needed the soothing oblivion of sleep. He got a large glass of water from the kitchen and went into his room. He took out his bottle of sleeping pills and lay down on the bed.

When Judy called by two hours later she knew Jamie was home because the house was so well lit. She rang the doorbell. When Jamie did not answer she grew frightened. She banged on the door and called out his name but he failed to respond. She ran around the house, pulling at windows, trying all the doors but the house was locked and she could not get inside. In a state of panic she rang the doorbell of the house next door and asked to use the phone. Her body was shaking and her fingers fumbled as she dialled the number of the nearest police station. The police only took five minutes to get there. They forced their way in and Judy led them to Jamie's bedroom. His breathing was harsh and irregular. An empty bottle of sleeping pills lay beside him on the bed.

CHAPTER 5

'I didn't try to kill myself,' said Jamie. 'I had a bad arthritic attack. The pain was so intense that it drove me out of my mind. I took painkillers but they didn't work. I decided that the only thing to do was to take enough sleeping pills to be sure that I slept. If I could get to sleep then I hoped I might be over the worst of the attack by the time I woke up. The pain clouded my judgement. I took more sleeping pills than I intended to take. I didn't try to kill myself.'

This was the story that Jamie told the young intern in Emergency after they had pumped out his stomach and brought him back to consciousness. It was the story that he told his friend Judy when they allowed her in to see him. She had come with him in the ambulance and had sat outside, anxiously awaiting news of his condition. It was the story he told his mother, who rushed back from Canberra as soon as she was contacted, and his father, who had gone to his beach house but cut his weekend short to get to Jamie's bedside. None of them believed him. The registrar in Emergency insisted that he be moved to a ward for a few days' observation. If he were allowed to go home immediately, he might attempt suicide again. He needed to be assessed by a psychiatrist and he should talk to one of the social workers.

Jamie refused to cooperate, demanded to be released, and stuck to his story. He repeated it so many times over the next few days that he came to believe it himself. When he had regained consciousness in Emergency, with the glaring lights above him and the anxious faces of nurses and doctors hovering on either side of him, to hear someone say, 'He's coming round! He's going to be alright!', he'd felt a surge of joy at the realisation that he was still alive. He was glad he had failed and he pushed that terrible moment of dark despair so far back into his mind that he made it disappear altogether. His spirit soared and it seemed as if he had, momentarily, transcended the physical bondage of his body. How extraordinarily powerful was the will to live; how unfettered and free was the human soul. In that moment of exaltation he was determined that he would not be conquered. He would grasp hold of his life, however meagre and worthless it may appear to others. He would fulfil his potential, even though that potential was so severely limited by his physical condition. It was a euphoric moment. A taste of ecstasy. And although the feeling did not last, he held onto its meaning, kept its message clearly etched in his mind. He did not communicate this moment of insight to anyone else, believing that the glory of the experience would be somehow tarnished if he tried to share it with others. He did, however, appear to be both cheerful and optimistic and, as he exhibited no symptoms of depression, they agreed to discharge him after two days.

The first thing he did when he got home was to hire a small removal truck, together with a driver. It was mid-morning when they arrived at the studio. He told the removal man to double park the truck and come inside with him.

'I'm not waiting for the auction,' said Jamie, as he entered the studio. 'I'm taking my things now.' And he gave directions to the man, pointing out what he wanted removed. He took the wheel he was accustomed to using, two small decorating wheels, a pug mill machine, cutting wire, various decorating tools, glazes, a large quantity of clay and any of his own pottery that was stacked on the shelves in the shop area. Jamie conducted the removal with such authority that no one had any inclination to object. His demeanour was calm and there was an air of invulnerability about him. He did not appear to be either angry or hurt. He was simply taking what he considered was rightfully his. If anyone thought that he should, really, have taken only one decorating wheel and that, strictly speaking, he could not regard the pug machine as his own property, no one said so. He was in and out of the studio in less than an hour and felt a joyous sense of liberation as the removal truck took him back home. He would have to store his equipment in the garage for the time being, until he decided where he was going to set up his own studio.

It was not healthy for him to be living at home with his mother. She was, of course, kind and good but she was his mother and he felt restrained and restricted by her presence. He had to pretend too much. He wanted to be able to swing from joy to despair, if he felt like it, without needing to consider how she would react to his mood changes. She was always watching him, trying to ascertain his state of mind, hoping to anticipate pain or hurt in order to cushion him from the inevitable blows that life dealt him. In the end her concern irritated him and he found himself snapping at her, unfairly he thought, considering that she was doing everything in her power to please him. He ought to get away from her.

Although there were disadvantages in communal living, Jamie thought that, on the whole, the three years he'd spent as a member of Jessica's household, while he was attending college, had been very satisfying in terms of living arrangements. One alternative was to use the garage as a studio and to live in a communal household. He was reluctant, however, to simply answer some advertisement and take a room among people he knew nothing about. And, if he were being honest with himself, he had to admit he was afraid of rejection. What if he were turned away because of his physical handicap? He did not think he could bear that. He had come to believe that the city itself was alienating. He felt isolated and he did not know how to go about making new acquaintances. More and more, his thoughts turned to Jessica, living up there in the Blue Mountains, comfortably secure in the warm environment of an art and craft community. Although he had not seen her for over two years, he had her address and phone number. When he rang she sounded pleased to hear from him. He asked whether he could come and see her. She hesitated for a moment but then she invited him up.

'We've got a spare room,' said Jessica. 'You could come and stay with us next weekend, if you like. Come on Friday night. And make sure you bring a thick, woolly jumper. It's not too bad during the day but it gets terribly cold at night.'

Jamie was highly optimistic. Jessica was his friend. She had always been supportive. She would introduce him to other members of her community. He would find himself among caring people with concerns and interests similar to his own. They would accept him, just as Jessica had always accepted him. He would find a place among them.

Jessica's house was outside of Leura, on an isolated road and set in a rugged landscape. When he arrived, Jamie was welcomed by Jessica and introduced to a tall, bearded man called John. Although John's hair and beard were completely white, his face was smooth and youthful. Jamie thought he might be in his early fifties.

'John just has to go and pick up his daughter from the railway station,' said Jessica. 'She comes up every Friday to spend the weekend with us. We'll have dinner when they get back.'

John left immediately and Jamie expressed his enthusiasm for the view, the house and the marvellous, bracing, mountain air.

'The house isn't mine, James. It belongs to John but we live here together. I suppose you'll find it strange that I've changed so much. You know what I was like. No commitment. A new lover every few months. But I fell in love with John the moment I met him and I've been in love with him ever since. I can't imagine how I ever lived without him. He's a painter. A very successful one. His studio is up here, next to the lounge room and he built me that shed down there beside the house. I have everything I need there for my work. You can't imagine how happy I am.'

'He looks a good bit older than you,' said Jamie.

'I've just turned forty, James. Can you believe that? He's thirteen years older than I am but perhaps that's what I needed. Those younger men of mine had great bodies but John's a better lover than any of them. Anyway, tell me about yourself. I hear things didn't work out too well for you at the cooperative.'

'Have you been speaking to Sean and Michael?'

'We keep in touch,' said Jessica.

'I want to come up here, Jessica, to live and work,' said Jamie.

'It mightn't be the right place for you. It doesn't suit every-one,' said Jessica.

'It would suit me,' said Jamie. 'I know it would.'

'Take my advice and don't make a decision too quickly,' said Jessica. 'I'll show you around, introduce you to a few people but you need to be absolutely certain that you'd fit in here. It's a very close community. If you didn't fit in, life would be hell.'

John's daughter, Angela, looked about sixteen years old. When she came through the door, Jamie was immediately stuck by the impression of naive innocence that she displayed.

Her long, blonde hair was loosely braided into a plait, which almost reached her waist. Her pretty, heart-shaped face was free of make-up. On entering the house, she took off her black, ankle length cloak, her heavy jumper and her boots. She stood in front of the open fire to warm herself. A vision in white. She was dressed in Indian style clothes made of cheesecloth - a floor length skirt and loose, long-sleeved shirt. Around her waist she wore a very thin, leather belt. The leather strips, which had been plaited to make the belt, were then left to hang half way down the length of her skirt, the ends tied off with coloured beads. She wore two long strings of fine wooden beads around her neck.

'Don't mind Angela, James,' said John, with an amused, affectionate glance at his daughter. 'She belongs to the new age. The flower children. Peace and love. They're going to save the world. They're sweeping America, my daughter claims, and they're getting ready to take over here. Hippies, I think they're called. Is that right, Angela?'

'Stop teasing, Daddy,' said Angela. 'When you were my age you were a left wing bohemian. You liked to think you were going to change the world. And look at you now. I'd say your life's turned out to be pretty tame and conventional.'

Jamie soon found out that Angela was older than she looked. She was, in fact, twenty, lived with her mother and was doing her third year of an Arts degree at Sydney University. During dinner she devoted herself exclusively to her father and they conducted their conversation as if Jessica and Jamie were not there. It was clear that their relationship was close and that they were very fond of one another. Jessica did not appear to be bothered by this and turned her attention to Jamie.

The next day, Jessica took Jamie to every craft shop in the Blue Mountains and to several private workshops. She introduced him to her fellow artists. Everyone he met was polite to him and they were willing and eager to explain their particular craft to him. He was especially interested in the ceramics made by an older woman called Ella. She specialised in miniature sized vases and plates that were intended only as ornaments. They were decorated with delicate, intricate designs. He seemed so intrigued that she invited him to come back, on his own, the following morning. They could have a cup of coffee and talk about pottery at greater length. As far as Jamie was concerned, the day had been a complete success. He was enthusiastic about everything he had seen and everyone he had met.

That evening Jessica and John had been invited out for dinner with friends and intended taking Jamie with them but Angela had different ideas. 'What does he want to go with you for? Your friends are ancient. He'll be bored. Why doesn't James drive me to the party at Mount Victoria? Then you won't have to worry about me.'

Jessica was hesitant but Angela was used to getting her own way and Jamie, without ever being asked which alternative he would prefer, found himself allocated the task of chauffeuring Angela to and from the party. It seemed that Angela's group of friends managed to find a venue for a party almost every Saturday night. They looked for houses that were, for one reason or another, free of parental control for the weekend. This was necessary because the purpose of the party was to put into practice the philosophy of the members of the group. They believed in smoking marijuana, playing appropriate music, and allowing the mind-expanding effects of the cannabis to determine the direction of the evening. This might lead to nothing more than the sharing of newly acquired insights into life but it could lead to the true sharing of brotherhood and understanding by means of love making. Make love, not war, was, after all, a primary tenet that they all held dear.

There were about twenty-five people at the party and Jamie judged that most of them were in their late teens to early twenties. Their dress was like a uniform - long skirts and blouses for the girls, baggy pants and Indian shirts for the boys. The young men wore their hair loose, at shoulder length and favoured shaggy, Jesus-like beards. Jamie felt out of place with his short hair, his jeans and polo-neck jumper. He also felt out of place because of his age. He was clearly the oldest person there. Although there was probably not more than a ten year age gap, he felt that he belonged to an entirely different generation. They were, however, kind and welcoming and by the time he had taken several puffs of the joints that were being passed around, he was comfortably able to see himself as their brother. He was disconcerted to find himself giggling for no reason but when he realised that everyone else was doing the same thing he allowed himself to laugh whenever he felt like it. He became enormously hungry, even though he'd eaten a large dinner, but that also seemed to happen to everyone else and he was relieved when someone brought out packets of biscuits, cakes and jars of nuts and dried fruit. They washed the food down with gallons of orange juice. Some couples fondled each other and, despite the cold weather, a few of the girls took off their shirts and bras. The sexual caresses and the bare breasts seemed so natural to Jamie that he was in no way shocked or surprised. Indeed he felt so utterly at peace with his fellow man that he simply sat back and allowed the goodwill of others to flow over him. By the time the party ended, the effects of the marijuana had worn off and Jamie returned to his feeling of being quite out of place. He had, however, shared a moment of oneness with others and for that he was grateful.

'Thanks for letting me take you to the party,' he said to Angela, as he drove her home. 'It was a great experience.'

'You won't tell Daddy, will you? If he knew I was smoking dope he'd give me a hard time,' said Angela.

'Don't worry,' said Jamie. 'I'll keep it to myself.'

'Thanks,' said Angela. 'This car of yours is fantastic. Can I come back to Sydney with you tomorrow afternoon? I'd love to feel what it's like when you drive it on the open road."

'Of course,' said Jamie.

The next morning he visited Ella and they talked for hours about her work. She showed him how she made her miniatures. She knew that most potters loved the craft because they were creating beautiful objects that were functional but she did not feel that way. She simply wanted her work to be admired. By the time he left her, he was sure that he had made a friend. John took them out for a long, late, lazy lunch at a quaint restaurant in Katoomba. It had been a perfect weekend. Jamie got his things together, ready to leave with Angela.

As they were about to get into the car, Angela turned to her father and Jessica. 'If James came to stay again next weekend, he could drive me up here and then take me back to Sydney.' James could see that both Jessica and John were hesitating. 'Please,' said Angela. 'It would be so nice not to have to catch the train.'

'Alright,' said John. 'We'll see you both next Friday night.'

The second weekend at the mountains proved to be as delightful as the first. Jamie spent very little time with Jessica and John because Angela insisted that he drive her wherever she wanted to go. Although it was the middle of May and the weather ought to have been cold, this weekend it was extremely hot during the day. On the Saturday morning, Angela asked Jamie to drive her and a few friends to a favourite, secluded spot where they wanted to swim in a pool that lay beneath a small waterfall. It was certainly a beautiful place. Firstly they lay around in the sun until they were warm enough to take their clothes off to swim. Angela and her two friends, one male and one female, disrobed unselfconsciously and jumped into the pool, laughing, splashing and climbing up the rocks to stand under the waterfall. How envious Jamie felt of their young, perfect bodies.

'You can't just watch, James,' said Angela. 'You have to come in.'

'No,' said Jamie, 'I don't think so.'

'You have to,' insisted Angela. 'I want you to.'

So Jamie took off his clothes as quickly as he could and slipped into the pool. How wonderful it was! To be swimming naked with two beautiful young women. How idyllic life would be when he came to the mountains to live. There was, however, an unpleasant moment as they were all getting out of the pool. Jamie turned suddenly and splashed Angela with water. She was not expecting him to do anything like that and she immediately grew angry.

'What did you do that for?' said Angela.

'Just for fun,' said Jamie.

'Well, I don't think it was very funny,' said Angela.

'But you were all splashing each other. Is there one rule for the three of you and a separate one for me?' asked Jamie.

His comment embarrassed Angela. She laughed uncomfortably and ignored Jamie while the four of them dried and dressed. She became friendly again when Jamie offered to take them all for a drive for the afternoon and she was pleased to have him escort her to a party in Katoomba that night. On Sunday he drove her to visit friends and when they left to return to Sydney late that afternoon, she did not ask whether Jamie could stay again the following weekend; she simply assumed that he would do so.

Jamie harboured no romantic illusions about Angela. Their discussions were friendly during the hours they spent together in the car but Angela made it clear that she had no intention of forming a serious relationship with anyone in the foreseeable future. She intended going overseas when she finished her degree and had no idea whether she would ever come back. Meanwhile, however, she seemed to like him and see him as a friend. She enabled him to meet young people who could provide him with social contacts when he moved to the mountains permanently.

It was during the third weekend that he began to look for somewhere to live. His father had agreed to subsidise his living expenses but he was not prepared to pay for Jamie to rent a house by himself. He would, therefore, have to look for shared accommodation. His first approach was to Jessica.

'How would you feel about renting me your spare room for a while,' said Jamie, 'and letting me share your studio until I get established up here?'

'I'm sorry, James, that wouldn't work. John and I have created a very harmonious, weekday working pattern. We'd find it disturbing to have anyone else in the house,' said Jessica.

Jamie took himself off to visit several of the people Jessica had introduced him to. He reminded them that he was a potter, that he was very keen to join the mountains arts community, that he was looking for shared accommodation and somewhere to work. Did they have any space? Did they know of anyone else who had suitable premises to offer him? He was disappointed to find that no one wanted to help him. He went back to visit Ella, the older woman potter whom he thought of as a friend, but she had difficulty actually remembering who he was and she certainly didn't know of anyone who would be willing to take him in.

By Saturday evening, he was quite despondent but he said nothing to Jessica. When he came up next weekend he'd visit a few estate agents and see what was available. If the people in the arts community weren't going to help him, then he'd have to help himself. He'd been too busy to spend any time with Angela during the day but he expected to be taking her to a party that night. She came out of her room, dressed and ready to go, but she ignored Jamie and turned to her father.

'Will you drop me over to Blackheith, Dad? There's a party on there tonight.'

'Of course,' said John. 'I'll just get my coat.'

'But I can take you, Angela,' said Jamie.

'No,' said Angela. 'No, you can't.'

'I don't mind,' insisted Jamie. 'I'd be happy to take you there.'

'But I mind,' said Angela. 'I mind very much. My friends think I'm interested in you. They think I'm involved with you. All day today they kept teasing me. No matter how much I denied it. It's too much. I can't bear them to think that I'd have an affair with a ....'

'With a cripple,' said Jamie.

'I didn't say that,' said Angela.

'But that's what you meant, isn't it? It's a wonderful philosophy you have, Angela. Love and peace. Understanding and tolerance. Free love for all - except cripples,' said Jamie.

'Come along, Angela,' said John. 'Let's go.' As they were leaving he turned back to Jamie. 'If you're coming up to the mountains next weekend, James, then you'll have to find somewhere else to stay.'

'I'm sorry, James,' said Jessica. 'I'm really sorry.'

'I'll get my things. I'll drive back tonight,' said Jamie.

'Stay tonight. You're upset now. You shouldn't drive. You can leave first thing in the morning,' said Jessica.

'That's impossible. The whole thing's impossible, isn't it, Jessica? Another rebuff. Another rejection. No one wants me here.'

'Your need is too great, James. You try too hard. You're too hungry for acceptance. It puts people off. I don't know what to say to you,' said Jessica.

'I think you've said enough.' He packed up his things and left immediately. As he drove back to Sydney, he thought about Jessica's words. She didn't understand. No one did. He wanted so little. Just a touch, a kind word, a gesture of friendship. Why was it so difficult for people to accept him? He was good-hearted, kind and loving. Why couldn't they see beyond his physical disabilities? He was rejected by the very people who would have claimed they were not prejudiced. They would have said that they treated all their fellow human beings as equals and yet they turned away from him. Jessica was wrong, quite wrong. It was not his own behaviour that alienated others. It was others who were to blame. It was impossible for people to tolerate his physical imperfection. It was late when Jamie arrived home and Elizabeth, who had not been expecting him, jumped out of bed to find out what was wrong.

'Nothing's wrong. It didn't work out, that's all. The whole Blue Mountains idea. I won't be going to live there,' said Jamie. 'I'll be staying here. I'll use the garage as a studio for a while.' Elizabeth moved towards him, putting out her arms as if to hold and comfort him but he turned away angrily. 'Don't look at me like that! I can't stand your pity. Go back to sleep. There's nothing you could do or say that would help me.' He was exhausted from the long drive home. Pain was gnawing into his joints. He needed painkillers and sleeping pills. Tomorrow he'd worry about the future.

The garage was badly lit and he could only work there with the door open. Winter had begun and the days were windy and cold. He worked at his wheel clad in heavy jumpers, a scarf around his neck, a woollen beanie pulled down over his ears. The cold numbed his hands, making it more and more difficult for him to achieve the shapes that he envisaged. It took such effort to create a pot he was pleased with that he began to wonder if it was all worthwhile. Two or three hours a day were all that he could tolerate.

He had no kiln and he had no outlet to sell his work. Both these problems had to be solved if he intended to continue working as a potter. He did not know where to turn because he felt he had to shun any former colleagues who had hurt him or rejected him in any way. Then he remembered the woman potter in Balmain, the one who had been so kind to him before he'd begun the course at college. She'd allowed him to spend a month with her, observing her work. He went to see her and explained his problem. She said that, if he did not have too many pieces to be fired, he could bring them over and she'd put them in the kiln whenever she had the space. It would be a nuisance, driving back and forth to Balmain, but it solved the problem of not having a kiln of his own. She also had a suggestion to make concerning selling his work. A friend of hers ran a pottery stall at Paddington markets every Saturday. Several potters brought their work to her and if she liked the kind of thing he was doing, she'd probably take him on.

The following Saturday, Jamie visited the Paddington markets. Set in the grounds of a church, the markets, even in winter, were crowded and lively, packed with stalls selling such a variety of original and individually made goods that Jamie was enchanted. There were clothes of outrageous design, hand-painted T-shirts, leatherwork, hand-made jewellery. When he found the pottery stall he introduced himself to the women working there. The older woman, Pam, was obviously in charge and her daughter, Julie, was there as a helper. Jamie asked Pam if she would be willing to sell his pottery.

'Have you brought anything with you?' asked Pam.

'Just a few things,' said Jamie, taking off his small backpack. 'I thought parking would be a problem and I can't carry much if I have to walk long distances.'

Pam had already noted Jamie's metal walking sticks and she took the backpack from him, undid it and removed the three pieces he had brought with him. She unwrapped them carefully. There was one small vase, a fruit bowl and a coffee mug.

'These are just examples of the kind of thing I make,' said Jamie. 'I've got quite a bit of stock at home that I'd like to sell. And, of course, I'm trying to work every day. I'm not producing very much at the moment. My hands are quite painful during the winter.'

'Yes,' said Pam. 'I like these. I think they'd sell. I'll give you my address at home. Most of my potters deliver their work to me, wrapped and in boxes, and then we bring it here every Saturday morning. I charge 30% commission. I know that sounds a lot but it's the only way I can make any money. Is that alright with you?'

'That's fine,' said Jamie and he went away feeling well pleased with himself.

Although he had, for the moment, solved the problems associated with his work, Jamie found little satisfaction in his day to day life. The attempt to work, even for a few hours a day, caused a great deal of pain. When he looked at his hands, it seemed to him that the joints were becoming more grotesquely deformed every day. He hoped it was just the winter weather but what if it wasn't? What if his hands deteriorated further, to the point of making it impossible for him to work at all? He was plagued by that possibility even though he tried to push it away as too cruel to contemplate.

He was isolated and lonely. Sometimes he met his friend Judy for dinner. He went to the movies with his mother. He visited his father every few weeks. He talked to the potter at Balmain when he took his work over to be fired and he chatted to Pam and Julie when he delivered his pottery to their house. That was all. It was not enough.

There were many hours when Jamie was alone and in those hours he thought about life and how he might go about improving the quality of his own particular life. He looked up into the sky and contemplated the universe and he knew that, theoretically, his life was only an eye-blink in eternity and yet, it was surely reasonable to want to make one's short time of existence meaningful. He knew that people like himself often found solace in religion, believing that a higher being was watching over them and caring about them in times of trouble. When he looked at the universe he thought it possible that there might be a Designer but the idea that this Designer could be concerned with the plight of one small earth being called Jamie Liebler was ludicrous, ridiculous. Nevertheless, there were people who believed that this was so and those people professed to care about their fellow men. Jamie began to wonder if such people could care about him. There was a group of people at a Chapel in the city who were often in the news. They offered comfort to everyone, to prostitutes and drug addicts, to gamblers and alcoholics, to criminals and street kids. Perhaps, Jamie thought, they might offer comfort to him. He thought he might go along and give them a try.

He went there on a weekday afternoon. He thought perhaps they wouldn't be so busy at that time and he was right because a counsellor, who introduced herself as Gillian, was the only person in attendance when he arrived. She smiled at Jamie and held out her hand to him as she welcomed him. She did not let go of his hand and she did not ask him why he was there; she simply said, 'I'm so pleased that you've come to us, James. I have a small office, just through here. We can talk in there very comfortably without any fear of interruption.'

She led him into her office, sat him down on an old two-seater lounge and sat herself down beside him. She was still holding his hand in a warm, firm grasp. She turned towards him, looked at him with steady, unblinking, compassionate eyes and said, 'How can I help you, James?'

'How do you know that I need help?' said James.

'Everyone who comes here needs help,' she replied.

'I don't know where to begin,' said James.

'Why don't you start by telling me how you feel about your-self at the moment. Take your time. There's no rush.'

He began hesitantly. Initially it was embarrassing to be sitting there telling a stranger his innermost thoughts but she did seem sincere. She wanted to listen to him and he wanted to unburden himself. Soon all the years of pain and sorrow and rejection came tumbling out. He gave her his loneliness, his isolation, his lack of love and she responded by taking them into herself. He felt that she had emptied herself of her own concerns in order to be able to receive his. She gathered his pain into her heart and held it there. The relief of being able to transfer it to someone else was so great that he found himself crying. She allowed him the luxury of uncontrolled weeping and did nothing to restrain his outburst. When it was over she let go of his hand and walked over to her desk to get a large box of Kleenex tissues.

'I'm sorry,' said Jamie, as he wiped his eyes and blew his nose.

'Don't be,' said Gillian. 'You've kept your feelings contained for too long.'

'But telling you everything, as I've done today, isn't going to solve my problems. I feel better, of course I do, but I still have this useless, crippled body that no one can love. I can't escape that and I don't know how to live with it,' said Jamie.

'Everyone who comes here is crippled, James,' said Gillian. 'You're not the only one. Sometimes people are damaged in ways that are not observable to others. They're so emotionally crippled that they feel condemned to life without love. But they come here and many of them are healed. They're able to go on from here and lead happy, meaningful lives.'

'But how? How do you save people?'

'I was an alcoholic when I first came here for help five years ago and now I spend my life helping others. You can come here any time of the day or night, James. There will always be someone here to comfort you. That's the most important thing. And those of us who help you gain our strength and our compassion from a belief that God is directing us in our work.'

'That's a problem for me,' said Jamie. 'I don't believe in that sort of God.'

'Neither did I, in the beginning,' said Gillian,' but after you've been coming here for a while you can't help being influenced by the fact that a belief in God gives people the courage to go on. You're welcome here, whether you believe or not. We don't force people to attend our chapel services but if you do attend them you might find the experience rewarding. Meanwhile you can help yourself by helping others.'

'What do you mean?' said Jamie.

'We provide a meeting place here,' said Gillian. 'Any evening in the week you'll find people gathered here. They're all in trouble of some kind. They all need help and understanding. Come as often as you please. Come with an open heart and an open mind. Listen to others. Speak to others. Hear their stories. Tell your own. You'll find that you're not alone, James. You told me, a short while ago, that one of the things that saddens you most is that you believe you have a great deal to give and yet people seem unwilling to accept what you want to give to them. That won't happen here, James. What you give to others will be gratefully received and by giving you'll enrich your life.'

Jamie began to spend a great deal of his time at the Chapel and he found that what Gillian said was true. It did enrich his life. He did not attend Chapel services but he did admire, and even envy, those who found hope in belief. What he gained was perspective. Although his body was twisted and deformed, both his mother and his father had loved him. He realised what a blessing that had been when he listened to the tales of abuse and deprivation suffered by others. At the Chapel he did indeed feel that he could love and be loved as a human being. He did, however, have reservations. He had taken a step down into the world of the severely damaged. To be accepted by them was an acknowledgment of his failure to be accepted by what he regarded as the normal world. And to be loved as a human being was not the same thing as being loved as a man. He still longed for, and was denied, the individual, intimate love of some particular woman.

Winter passed and with the coming of spring Jamie felt that his state of mind was in harmony with the change of seasons. No more dark, negative thoughts. Attending the Chapel had contributed to his state of mental well-being. He had come to know people who were now dear to him. He gave them his time, he gave them his love and he felt, at last, that they acknowledged the love he had to give. Spring would pass and turn into summer. This summer he would celebrate his thirtieth birthday. He felt confident now that he would live beyond his thirtieth year even though his body was deteriorating. The warmer weather had brought no relief to his misshapen hands and work was difficult and frustrating. His lungs were painful and often each breath was a struggle for survival. Sometimes, when he felt too ill to work, he was quite content to sit at home, dreaming of the pots he would create if only he were physically able to do so. He still believed that if he had a true mate, a woman to love and live with, then his pain would be eased and he would, miraculously, be set free to move forward into creative, productive life.

There was a girl at the Chapel for whom Jamie felt a particular sympathy. She was so withdrawn that, for many weeks, she could not communicate with anyone. She attended Chapel gatherings regularly. Indeed she always seemed to be there, as if she had nowhere else to go. She would sit on a chair, her legs drawn up, arms clutched tightly around her knees. She watched others as they spoke and perhaps she was listening to what they had to say. It was difficult to know. There was about her an air of such profound melancholy that no one doubted the existence of her inner despair. Although everyone was kind to her, she was quite unable to respond. Jamie was determined to break through the barriers she had constructed to defend herself. He wanted to win her confidence. He wanted to become her friend.

It was not easy. Every time he saw her he would spend at least half an hour sitting in a chair beside her. He did not look at her directly and he never asked her anything about herself. He talked about himself. He recalled the most painful of his life experiences and he presented them to her in minute detail. He conjured up examples of rejection, humiliation, unkindness and prejudice. He told her of his debilitating illness, describing its progress and prognosis. When he had finished recounting a particular incident, he would remain seated beside her, in silence, for several minutes, hoping for a response. He had to wait three weeks for his reward. One evening she broke the silence by turning to him and saying, 'My name's Vicki,' and she followed the words with a brief, tentative smile.

Vicki was twenty-two although her thin, child-like body and her timid, withdrawn behaviour combined to make her appear much younger. She was, at the moment, living in a women's refuge, having somehow found the courage to escape from a brutal home life. Her mother, a single parent, was an alcoholic who had been totally unable to offer her daughter any protection or support. For years Vicki had been subjected to regular sexual abuse by her two older brothers. She was only prepared to give Jamie a brief outline of what had happened to her. In fact it took less than five minutes for her to summarise her life history.

'And I don't want to talk about this any more,' she added. 'I just want to forget about it.'

Jamie began to take her on outings - drives in the countryside, picnics, restaurants for lunch. He took her home to show her his pottery. He tried to teach her how to use the wheel but she had no inclination to learn. He endeavoured to broaden her horizons by taking her to museums and art galleries and to intellectually challenging movies. He gave her books that he hoped she would read. She was willing and eager to go anywhere that he suggested but she seemed to be incapable of learning anything. Her attitude to all she was exposed to was childlike wonder but, unlike a child, she did not absorb knowledge from what she was witnessing. Jamie found this frustrating. He knew that her horrific family background had left her traumatised and he wanted to be the one to save her. In Vicki he had, at last, found a woman who was so hurt, so damaged and so helpless that she would certainly be grateful to him for rescuing her. He gave all his time and attention to winning her confidence in the sure knowledge that he would, eventually, be able to lead her back to normality.

Love was the answer. Love was the way. He would declare his love for Vicki. He would offer to marry her. She would have comfort, protection, financial security, a home of her own. He would look after her forever. Their love would conquer any obstacles that stood in their way. They would face life fearlessly together.

Walter and Elizabeth had arranged a lavish family gathering to celebrate Jamie's thirtieth birthday and Jamie was determined to announce his engagement to Vicki on the night of the party. It would be a grand gesture to declare his own confidence in his own future on such a night. He approached Vicki with the absolute certainty that she would agree to his suggestion.

'But I can't marry you, James,' said Vicki. 'You're my friend.'

'I know I'm your friend but friendship can grow into love, can't it?'

'I do love you,' said Vicki. 'I really do but not in the way I'd need to love someone I married. I hope one day that I'll be able to love a man in that way. I hope I'll get over what's happened to me so that I'll be able to live with a man but it couldn't be you. I'm sorry. I'm truly sorry but it couldn't be you.'

Jamie did not allow Vicki to see that her refusal had numbed him with disappointment. Her weakness had given him confidence and strength and now he had to face rejection. Once again he must be a witness to his own failure to make another person happy. If Vicki could not accept his love then perhaps there was no hope that any woman could ever love him.

'You've helped bring me back to life, James,' said Vicki. 'I'll never forget that. I'll always want to be your friend. You're the kindest, nicest person I've ever known. And I hope, I really hope that you'll find the right girl one day, someone who can love you the way you deserve to be loved.'

'But I wanted you to love me that way,' said Jamie.

'You're not really in love with me, James. You just want to be in love with me and wanting something doesn't make it real.'

'But I am in love with you and I'm sure that, if you let yourself, you could learn to love me,' said Jamie.

'No, James, that's not true. Anyway, I didn't come to the Chapel looking for love. I came for help. And I found it. If I ever find love it won't be with anyone I've met here. It will be someone else, someone from out there in the real world.'

Vicki's rejection was painful but not as traumatic as it might have been. There was no need to completely break off his relationship with her and her presence did not mean that he had to give up attending gatherings at the Chapel. However, his romantic hope of finding a suitable mate had, for the moment, been shattered. There was no point in continuing to go out with Vicki. He was polite and friendly towards her when he saw her but his visits to the Chapel became less frequent.

Pain, exhaustion and an increasing inability to get his hands to execute his envisioned designs had reduced Jamie's pottery output so drastically that he seldom found it worthwhile taking his work to Pam to be sold at Paddington markets. Often five or six weeks elapsed with nothing to show for his efforts. He did try to work for two or three hours each morning and the failure to work effectively was frightening. Physiotherapy and monitored exercise helped to maintain his present level of hand movement and, hopefully, might prevent further deterioration, but no amount of therapy was able to bring back the flexibility required for his work. He tried to be optimistic but it was difficult to deny the certainty that one day he would have to give up making his beloved pots. The idea that this inevitable day might arrive quite soon caused depression and despair. What would he do with his life if he had to abandon the creative path he'd chosen to follow? He discussed his fears with Pam the next time he saw her, told her that he didn't know how much longer he'd be able to go on with his work. She was kind, sympathetic and she had a proposition to put to him.

'My daughter, Julie, doesn't really want to work with me at the markets any more. She's helped me for years and she's pretty fed up with the whole thing. To tell you the truth, James, I'm getting a bit tired of it myself. Why don't you come and work with me on Saturdays for a while? See if you like it. You'd never be able to get a stall of your own there but if you worked with me for six months then you could just take over and I could ease my way out. The management committee would let you do that and you'd find yourself with an interesting business to run. If you have to give up making your own pots you mightn't be so upset about it if you've found something else to do. What do you think?'

'I think it sounds wonderful, Pam,' said Jamie. 'I can't wait to start.'

A new interest. A new direction. A new meaning to life. Jamie approached his work at the markets with enthusiasm and a great willingness to learn. He loved the atmosphere, the easy camaraderie that existed between the stallholders. Meeting as they did, only once a week, was an occasion for goodwill. Had they worked beside one another seven days a week, then differences and disagreements might have arisen but there was no time for pettiness or bickering. They were united in their desire for warmth, sunshine, large crowds and the need to sell as much merchandise as possible in the one day allotted to them. They were cooperative and friendly, minding each other's stalls when necessary, keeping an eye out for each other's welfare, recommending each other's wares. It was joyous working there and although the day was long, Jamie never felt tired or bored. He looked forward to the time when he would take over the stall himself and he began to develop ideas about improvements or changes he might make.

He could see, from the amount of money they took each Saturday, that it was possible to make a reasonable living from this one day's work. The idea that he could be financially self-sufficient, without having to depend on his father's weekly handouts, was very attractive to Jamie. How he longed to prove to Walter that he was not a failure, that he could make enough money to support himself.

When Jamie took over the stall, he needed someone to help him and the obvious person to employ was his mother. He remembered what an asset Elizabeth had been when they'd run the shop at Manly. She was very willing to join him. At the end of each Saturday Jamie would count out the money they'd taken, put aside the amount payable to the various potters who provided him with his merchandise, and then divided the remainder into two neat piles. He gave his mother one third of each day's profits and kept the rest for himself.

Jamie intended to sell pottery for the next six months and then to explore the possibility of changing to something more profitable. The stall next to his did a fantastic amount of business and he was very impressed with their success. They imported and sold goods from India - incense, oils, jewellery, ornaments, sandals, and saris. Jamie's idea was to run a similar business with imports from the Philippines. He was making inquiries and establishing contacts. The idea of setting up an import enterprise was exciting and challenging. When he felt ready he would go on a buying trip to the Philippines himself.

Meanwhile he devoted his efforts to making his Saturdays at the markets as profitable as possible.

The family who ran the Indian stall next to Jamie's were Buddhists. Although they were Australians, of Anglo-Saxon origin, they all wore Indian clothes, not the hippie variety but traditional saris for the women and pyjama suits for the men. There was the father, Brian, his wife, Margaret, their two sons, David and Paul and their daughter, Melanie. The three children were in their twenties and the parents appeared to be in their early fifties. Jamie was struck by the gentle, peaceful demeanour of the members of this family. They were especially kind and helpful to Jamie when he took over the stall. They could see how difficult it was for Jamie and his mother to unload the pottery from their cars and set up their stall. Right from the beginning, Brian insisted that his family should help in these tasks. Jamie wanted to manage everything by himself but each member of this extraordinary family insisted that it was a privilege to help another human being in this way. They made no reference to Jamie's physical shortcomings but it was clear that they saw it as their duty to come to the aid of someone who was physically less fortunate than themselves.

Jamie admired the whole family so much that he sought conversation with them at times when they were not too busy. He found each of them willing to discuss the family's beliefs and attitudes. They were pure vegetarians because they could not condone injury to any living creature. They believed that Buddhism, as a religion, was very simple and practical. Buddha had cut out all rites and rituals and had demonstrated the basic principles of righteous living by example. His teachings, Jamie was told, encouraged purity of heart, meekness and humility.

'You don't have to believe in God to be a Buddhist,' Brian told him. Jamie was willing to listen to the precepts of a religion that did not require belief in God as a premise. 'You see, James, unhappiness in this world stems from man's inability to control his desires. Desire is the root cause of our sufferings. We're greedy. We want too much and when we don't get what we want we're disappointed and unhappy. If we can control desire, we can eliminate unhappiness. So the greatest lesson Lord Buddha had to teach the whole world was that the path to freedom, the path to happiness, the path to nirvana starts from desirelessness. To be desireless is to be free from worry, free from wants and free from all worldly attachments.'

It sounded so simple. But was it possible? Could he, Jamie, learn to desire nothing? It was an attractive prospect.

'We follow the teachings of a particular guru,' said Brian. 'His name is Maharaj Ji. He comes to our house every Sunday afternoon to teach us and to pray with us. We have an open house. Everyone is welcome. Perhaps you'd like to join us one Sunday. If you become a member of the Buddhist faith you'll change your entire attitude to life, I promise you. You'll learn to meditate and meditation helps you to achieve serenity. Those things that trouble you right now will seem unimportant in a few months' time.'

Jamie decided to give it a try. If he could dismiss his desires then he would be happier. If he could transcend his crippled body and eliminate his yearning for physical love then surely his suffering would be diminished. He could see how peaceful each member of this Buddhist family seemed to be. He wanted what they had. He longed to be like them. So he went to their house on the first Sunday afternoon that he was free to do so.

The house was in Mosman, overlooking the harbour. It was a large house with wide, spacious verandahs and there must have been forty or fifty people there on the occasion of Jamie's first visit. Maharaj Ji was sitting cross-legged on a raised platform, at one end of the living area, waiting for his followers to arrive and settle down. He was an old man, with a long, wispy, grey beard, dressed only in a loin cloth and a turban. Brian and Margaret welcomed Jamie and instructed their daughter, Melanie, to look after him and find him somewhere comfortable to sit. Most people were sitting cross-legged on the floor. As that was impossible for Jamie, Melanie led him to a small two-seater lounge at the back of the room and sat down beside him.

'I'm so glad that you came, James,' said Melanie. She took his hand and squeezed it encouragingly before letting it go. She was sitting very close to him as Mahraj Ji began to speak.

'To have knowledge,' said Maharaj Ji, 'one should have only what one needs, not what one wants.' He paused and remained silent for a few minutes to allow his followers to absorb and assess the simple statement he had made. Then he went on. 'Music is made by instruments that catch the eternal melodies of the cosmos and transmit them so that they are audible to the ear. But the music is not created by the instrument. The instrument is just an instrument - nothing more. Just as the cosmic melodies are made audible for us, so we, through our bodies, transmit the true knowledge of the universe. The knowledge is there, just as the music is there. We are just an instrument to make the knowledge available to others who cannot hear it. Just as there are bad instruments there are imperfect people. But men originate from the cosmos and so it is possible to have a perfect being to speak the perfect knowledge, to spread the light of perfect love and understanding amongst others, others who themselves were not built so perfectly.'

Jamie found this a bit illogical and a touch too mystical for his liking but he noticed that many of the followers were nodding their heads or murmuring their agreement. It was clear that they saw their guru as one of the perfect products of the universe. Maharaj Ji went on. 'Beauty cannot be bought or sold. It cannot be created by man, for the judgement man puts on his creations is arbitrary. True beauty is eternal; it is man's knowledge of his cosmic consciousness and may be shown in his love for others, and a true understanding and joy of life.'

Jamie had real trouble coming to terms with a concept like 'cosmic consciousness'. He began to feel that he had wasted his time coming here. But then Maharaj Ji gave him something that he could really hold onto.

'True happiness cannot be found in material things. The only happiness is in the mind. Happiness, if it comes from within instead of relying on external objects, is completely satisfying. The strange thing is that we have been conditioned to believe that the more we have, the happier we are. But to achieve real happiness, the reverse applies. If our minds can achieve the state of no thoughts - to have it at the stage where it does not even relate to our bodies - then we are well on the way to achieving happiness. When we realise we can be perfectly happy when we meditate and become unaware of our physical existence, we realise the true nature of things. We must realise the unimportance of having 'the body beautiful' and the importance of having complete peace of mind. Let us meditate together.'

Yes, this is what Jamie wanted and in his desire to be free of bodily awareness he willingly joined Maharaj Ji's followers in meditation. After twenty minutes of perfectly silent meditation Jamie felt euphoric. He had been united with others in a journey of spiritual revelation. This was what he had been searching for. He was quite prepared to revere Maharaj Ji and to follow the path of his teachings.

For the next three months Jamie floated on a spiritual high. This was the way. Buddhism held the answers. He was even able to see himself as a small cog in the wheel of cosmic consciousness. He meditated morning and night. He experienced visions and revelations that he could not possibly have put into words. His spirit soared and traversed the cosmos, leaving his frail, deformed body behind. This was knowledge. This was freedom. And he was so enthusiastic about his new found faith that he felt compelled to talk about it, at length, to anyone who would listen to him. He harangued his mother for hours, trying to persuade her to join the faith so that she too could benefit from the knowledge of the meaning of life. Elizabeth listened but felt afraid for him. She tried to warn him that such wholehearted, ecstatic embracing of any religion could only result in disappointment.

Meanwhile the Buddhist family encouraged Jamie to join their movement. They invited him constantly to their home for dinner and discussion, prayer and meditation. It was Melanie, more than any other member of the family, who inspired him. When he looked into her face, glowing with fervour, he was so entranced that he felt his soul leap out of his body to join hers.

'We must realise our ultimate mission on earth, James,' she said. 'When we do that our love and devotion will benefit all mankind. We must fulfil the potential within ourselves.' He was swept along by her earnestness and swallowed up by the passion of her beliefs. And, inevitably, he was consumed by the knowledge that here, at last, was a woman worthy of his love - not mundane, sexual love but a love elevated to the high plain of spiritual worship.

At prayer meetings with Maharaj Ji, Jamie was sure that the dawn was beginning to break for all mankind. Maharaj Ji's face shone like the rising sun to cast a light on the cold, dark night of suffering. Man had fouled the world with polluted thoughts. Only through Maharaj Ji's knowledge could the earth be purified again. Jamie could glimpse the golden promised land and joined the thirsty souls who looked to their guru to show them the way to eternal happiness.

One day, after the Sunday afternoon meeting, Brian took Jamie aside and spoke to him. 'Well, James, you've been coming to our house for three months now. Do you feel ready to join our movement?'

'I thought I'd already joined it,' said Jamie.

'No, James. You have been enjoying the benefits of our faith but to be a member of our movement you must also accept a share of its responsibilities.'

'What responsibilities?' Jamie asked.

'Financial responsibilities,' Brian replied. 'We support the Maharaj Ji. We house, feed and clothe him. Pay for his trips overseas. This house that my family and I live in is owned by the movement. We need money for all those things. We need ongoing commitment. We need a substantial donation and then the agreement to pay 25% of your weekly earnings to the movement.'

'But you know my plans for the market stall,' said Jamie. 'I have to save as much as possible so that I can start to import goods from the Philippines. If I made a big donation, I couldn't carry out those business plans and, for the same reason, I couldn't give away such a large percentage of my earnings right now.'

'You have a very expensive car, James. You could donate that to us. It would be wonderful to have a car like yours at the Maharaj Ji's disposal,' said Brian.

Jamie was horrified at such a proposal. 'I'm not going to give you my car,' he said.

'Think about it, James. You'll have to give us something substantial,' said Brian.

'And if I don't?'

'Then I'm sorry to say that you'll no longer be welcome at our house,' Brian replied. 'And if you do decide to continue with us, I'll have to ask you to spend less time with Melanie. My daughter is not for you, James, not for you at all.'

Jamie was furious. So this was how he was to be treated! How insidious betrayal could be. They had seen how vulnerable he was. They had lured him into their religious movement. They were out to rob him of his money and his possessions and now, the ultimate insult - he was not good enough for their daughter. As soon as he arrived home he rang Melanie and asked her to meet him the next day for lunch.

'I don't think I'd be allowed,' said Melanie.

'I only want to talk to you. That's all,' said Jamie. 'They don't keep you as a prisoner. Just say you're going into town to do some shopping.'

'Alright. I'll come. But I don't feel right about it,' said Melanie.

'An hour of your time. That's all I need,' said Jamie.

When he met Melanie the next day, Jamie lost no time in exposing the falseness of her father and the greediness of the religious movement to which the family belonged. He pointed out what a hypocrite her father was. He professed meekness, humility and love for all mankind and yet he'd told Jamie to stay away from his daughter. What a mockery that made of the very fabric of their religious beliefs. 'You have to get out of there, Melanie. You're living a life based on hypocrisy and lies. You can come and live at our house. I'll look after you. I'll keep you safe and secure,' said Jamie.

'You're wrong, James. You can't see things clearly. Of course Maharaj Ji needs money to support him. It's our obligation to find it for him. A privilege to do so. It's our way of paying him back for the spiritual guidance he provides.'

'Does he need my car? Does he need a Jaguar for your father to drive him around in? Can't you see that it's all a sham? You're blind, Melanie, blind.'

'Then I'll stay blind,' she said, and she moved away from him, tears in her eyes.

'Melanie,' he called after her, 'Melanie! I'm only trying to help you.' If she heard his words she certainly took no notice of them. She did not look back but quickened her pace as if she wanted to get away from him as quickly as possible.

Jamie was angry and disillusioned. What a fool he'd been! Why did he continue to put his faith in the goodwill of others? Time and time again he'd put his trust in people only to find himself shunned and rejected. No. That wasn't quite true. His mother had never let him down and, on the whole, the people at the Chapel had offered him genuine acceptance. No more dependence on others. Self-reliance. That was the thing. He wasn't going to allow those hypocritical Buddhists to depress him. He could manage perfectly well without them.

The following Saturday morning Jamie and his mother set up the stall by themselves, refusing the embarrassed offers of help from the Buddhist family. They did not ignore each other entirely. Perfunctory pleasantries were exchanged. They did, after all, have to work beside each other every Saturday. Jamie worked hard at his stall and was pleased at how well he was doing. The money in the bank was growing steadily. Soon he'd have enough to make his planned business trip to the Philippines.

CHAPTER 6

It took a little longer than he'd anticipated for Jamie to save sufficient money for his Philippine venture. He wanted to be certain that he had adequate funds to ensure success without having to ask his father for any help. Walter would have helped because, at last, Jamie was undertaking what his father would have regarded as a viable business proposition but Jamie was determined to prove himself capable of financial independence. Elizabeth and Walter both came to the airport the day he left. Jamie was in a high state of excitement, eagerly anticipating the adventure of travelling overseas for the first time. His parents were fearful and anxious. What if he became ill? Who would look after him? How well trained were doctors in the Philippines? What were the hospitals like? Would Elizabeth, or Walter, be able to get to him quickly enough if he were in desperate need of help?

'I wish you'd stop worrying about me,' said Jamie. 'I can look after myself. I've got a suitcase full of medication. Pills for all occasions. I feel well. I feel strong. I'm going to have a great time.'

But he did not look either well or strong. Although running the stall at Paddington markets had done wonders for his morale and self-esteem, the steady decline of his body was clearly discernible. His fingers were now so twisted and deformed that he no longer attempted to work at his pottery. His hip joints had deteriorated to the point where it was impossible to walk anywhere without his metal walking sticks. Hip replacement operations had been suggested but Jamie's hatred of doctors and hospitals and his driving need to make a success of his business made him reluctant to undergo surgery,

173

with its inevitable lengthy period of rehabilitation. Walking required such enormous physical effort that his breathing was laboured, each breath taxing his weakened heart and lungs. It was impossible for him to leave the house without taking painkillers, impossible to sleep without sedatives. No wonder Elizabeth and Walter felt such apprehension about allowing their son to set off alone into unknown territory. There was, however, nothing they could do to stop him. Jamie was no longer a child. He was, after all, now thirty-one years old.

Jamie's confidence in his ability to travel overseas alone dwindled on arrival in Manila airport. The confusion, the crowds, the heat, the humidity caused momentary panic. He'd paid for a transfer to his hotel but what if no one turned up to meet him? What would he do? How would he cope? His hands were clammy, his face wet with sweat. He looked around anxiously. At last he found what he was looking for. A slender young man was holding high a card with the name 'Liebler', printed in capital letters. Jamie's heartbeat slowed and a grateful smile spread across his face as he made his way towards his saviour.

The trip to the hotel was a tedious bumper to bumper ride through traffic-blocked streets. Jamie made the mistake of winding down the window, hoping for a breath of fresh air. As soon as he did so, a woman ran up to the car, thrust her hand inside, begging for money. The driver laughed, shouted at the woman to go away and informed Jamie that it was unsafe to travel through Manila in a car with the windows down. Jamie was shocked. Every time the car stopped, which happened frequently, some man or woman or child would knock on Jamie's window, displaying pathetic goods for sale - chewing gum, cheap trinkets, packets of cigarettes - and holding out scrawny hands in the hope that Jamie might reward them with a few, meagre coins. The driver told Jamie to ignore them and further warned him not to go out on the streets wearing any kind of jewellery, not even his watch. He could easily be knocked down and robbed. So Jamie avoided looking at the beggars and, instead, found himself observing numerous brigades of workers, sweeping the roads with primitive brooms.

'Why do you have so many street cleaners,' Jamie asked.

'It's the way the government has of giving jobs to poor people. They earn very little,' said the driver, ' but it's better than nothing. Life is difficult here in Manila. You must be very careful.'

'I'm only staying overnight,' said Jamie. 'I'm going to Baguio in the morning.'

'Baguio. Oh, you'll be O.K. in Baguio. No problems for you there,' the driver assured him.

It was a relief to enter the air-conditioned, elegant hotel. By now it was late afternoon. Jamie had a shower, changed his clothes and then decided that he would, after all, be adventurous and go out for a short walk around the streets. Perhaps he would come across an interesting restaurant where he could eat an authentic Filipino meal. He hadn't gone more than a hundred metres when he changed his mind. He suddenly felt vulnerable. Everyone he passed looked like a potential criminal. What if he were pounced upon and robbed? How could he defend himself? Better to go back to the safety of the hotel. Eat at one of their restaurants. Have an early night. Be up bright and early for his flight to Baguio. Yes, that would be the best thing to do. No good taking risks. If anything bad happened to him in Manila, that would spoil his whole trip.

The city of Baguio was in Benguet province, a fifty-minute flight north of Manila. It was situated among pine-covered hills and valleys and there were two reasons why Jamie had chosen it as his destination. Firstly, it was famous for its markets which were said to be overflowing with handicrafts made by the mountain people from the surrounding highlands. Secondly, and this was something he had told no one about, Baguio was famous for its faith healing. Jamie knew that Baguio was the right place for him to purchase handicrafts for his Paddington market stall and he hoped that it might also be the right place for him to find a cure for his debilitating illness. He had seen a television program on the faith healers of Baguio and although the program implied that they were charlatans, Jamie could not get out of his mind the ecstatic joy on the faces of the patients who believed they had been cured. What good had conventional Western medicine ever done him? Why not try an alternative? It was, therefore, with fresh hope and high expectations that Jamie landed in Baguio. The sun was bright, the sky blue, the temperature pleasantly cool. He was met at the airport and driven through uncrowded streets to the attractive Baguio Hyatt hotel. Jamie was ready for his Philippine adventure to begin.

Jamie was enchanted by the hotel. If you looked up from the central reception area the floors of the hotel were arranged like graded terraces with a profusion of green plants growing on each level. There were two restaurants, a swimming pool and a few shops on the lobby level. Jamie decided to unpack, have an early lunch at the hotel's cafeteria-style restaurant and then take a taxi to the markets so that he could look at the handicrafts for himself. He intended to stay ten days in Baguio. That should be long enough to achieve his purposes as well as allowing him time to do some sightseeing. His mother had been willing to look after the market stall for two weeks on her own but he didn't want to burden her with any more responsibility than that.

Lunch was light, delicious and cheap and, from perusing the menu, Jamie could see that he'd be quite satisfied to eat his evening meal here as well. There'd be no need to patronise the more formal, expensive restaurant. Yes, it felt good to be in Baguio. With his spirits high he left the cafeteria and thought he might as well take a look at the handicrafts on offer at the hotel shop. He knew the prices would be inflated but, all the same, the person in charge of the shop might have some good advice for him. It was worth a try and he was in no hurry.

There was no one in the shop when he entered so he walked around, looking at the goods on display. There were intricately carved wooden boxes of all sizes, beautifully worked linen handkerchiefs, serviettes and tablecloths, embroidered shirts in a variety of colours and styles. He spent ten minutes or so closely examining the merchandise and then he became aware that someone had emerged from behind a screen at the back of the shop. A small, soft, female voice said, 'Can I help you?'

Jamie turned around and saw that the small voice belonged to a very small person. Although she was short, she was not a fragile girl. There was a solid, peasant quality in her build and her square face was framed by short, straight, black hair. A neat fringe came half way down her forehead. There was nothing sophisticated about her. She wore a very ordinary cotton frock and a long sleeved white cardigan.

Jamie looked at her and from the moment he laid eyes on her, he could not look away. Nor could he speak. He simply stared at her and she stared at him. Their eyes were locked in a mutual moment of surprise, acknowledgment, recognition. Nothing in Jamie's life had prepared him for this moment. And yet he knew exactly what it was. It was love. Love at first sight. And he knew that the look in the girl's eyes was a mirror image of his own. The thought flashed through his mind that he had never been in love before. He had wanted love, longed for love, believed he was in love but this moment, here and now, was positive proof that at last he understood what was meant by 'falling in love'. He was so intoxicated by the wonder of this extraordinary experience that he thought he might fall over in a faint at her feet. He didn't know what to do.

She reacted first. She tore her gaze away from his face and looked down, blushing in embarrassment. Her confusion created a similar response in him and he found himself burning with discomfort. He did not know what to say to her but he knew he had to say something to get them through the next few minutes.

'I'm from Australia,' he said, 'and I'm interested in your handicrafts. I don't want to buy anything here, from your shop, but I have a market stall of my own in Australia. I want to buy a lot of things and take them home with me to sell. Can you help me? Tell me where to go? Who to see?' And then he stopped. He couldn't think of anything else to say but it was enough. The girl had composed herself sufficiently to be able to take up the threads of the conversation, although she kept her eyes averted.

'Many members of my family have stalls at the main market. All kinds of things. I'm sure they can help. My name is Feli,' she said.

'And I'm James, James Liebler.'

'James. That's a very … I don't know … a very cold name. Here, in the Philippines, we use softer names. Are you always called "James"?'

'When I was a child I was known as "Jamie". My father still calls me that. He hasn't noticed that I've grown up. He still thinks of me as his little boy.'

Feli raised her eyes and allowed her warm, glowing smile to shine up into his face. 'Then I'll call you "Jamie". You'll be "Jamie" for me.' And the way she pronounced his name was as soft as a caress. 'Very soon one of my brothers will come to take his turn in the shop,' said Feli. English was obviously not her first language; her speech was slow and hesitant. 'When he arrives I'll send him to fetch my cousin, Marci. When she arrives we can go to the market and you can meet my relatives who will be able to help you.'

'Why can't we leave as soon as your brother gets here? We don't have to involve your cousin,' said Jamie.

'It would not be proper for me to go anywhere alone with you. My cousin Marci must be the … what do you call it?'

'Chaperone,' said Jamie. 'Really? Are you serious? Look at me. I'm not dangerous. You don't need anyone to protect you from me.'

'I am a Catholic girl, Jamie. My people are very religious, very … strict. I must have a chaperone at all times if I am with any man who might one day wish to marry me.'

'And do you see me, Feli, as a man who might one day wish to marry you?'

'Yes, of course, Jamie, of course. I felt that straight away, as soon as you first looked at me. I felt that there was between us a strong … a strong…'

'Attraction,' said Jamie.

'Attraction. Yes. That's what I felt. Forgive me if I am wrong. Perhaps I was mistaken,' and she looked down again in embarrassment.

'No, Feli, no. You weren't mistaken,' said Jamie. 'It's just that I think I'm so ugly. It seems almost impossible that you might …'

'Ugly? You are not ugly, Jamie. You have a beautiful face. Kind eyes. A sweet smile. I can tell that you are a good and loving man. That's what matters. Isn't that so?' Quite unexpectedly, tears began to roll down Jamie's cheeks. 'Why are you crying? I don't understand why you should be sad,' she said, as she pulled a handkerchief out of the sleeve of her cardigan and began to wipe his tears.

'They're tears of joy, Feli,' he said. 'I'm crying out of happiness because I've waited a long time to find someone who didn't think I was ugly.'

By the time cousin Marci arrived Jamie had learned quite a bit about Feli. She was twenty years old, the youngest child of a large family. Her people were members of the Benguet tribe. As her parents were both dead she lived with her only unmarried brother in a small house on the outskirts of the city market. She had several older brothers and sisters, all of whom were married with children. The family earned what they could by running market stalls but they were very poor. There was enough money to pay for food although their living conditions were appalling. It was difficult to afford clothes and shoes. The predicament of Feli and her family won his instant sympathy. Jamie elicited this information by asking direct questions and it did not escape his notice that Feli sought every possible opportunity to emphasise the poverty of her existence.

Once Marci had arrived and been introduced they set out to walk to the markets which were only a short distance away. The women were considerate and solicitous, adjusting their pace to suit Jamie's and stopping frequently when they could see that he was either in pain or out of breath. Marci dominated the conversation. She was in her mid-thirties, plump, good humoured, gregarious and obviously better educated than Feli. She was a widow, the mother of three children and worked as an English teacher at the local high school. She took pains to explain to Jamie that her salary as a teacher was inadequate. It did not even provide her with sufficient means to feed and clothe her children. Would the life of an Australian teacher be as difficult as hers? No, she was sure it wouldn't. How lucky Jamie was to have been born in an affluent country and not into the third world poverty of the Philippines. But she was an enterprising woman. She wasn't going to let her children starve. She'd started a small business of her own, organising the recruitment of women and girls to be sent to Hong Kong to work as domestics for wealthy Chinese families. These women were paid a fortune by Filipino standards and she was even thinking of going there herself for a few years to provide a nest egg for her children's future. If she did go, Feli would mind her children and, when she came back, Feli could go to Hong Kong for a few years. What alternative did a woman have? She either had to find a husband or make a living as best she could. It was no good sitting around, hoping that conditions in the Philippines would improve. They wouldn't. The country was riddled with corruption from top to bottom. She had to bribe officials to get passports for the women and girls she recruited, even though they had definite jobs to go to in Hong Kong.

Jamie did not know how to respond to Marci. Her outrage was genuine but was she venting her grievances with some specific purpose in mind? Did she expect him to help her in some way? Did she see him as an easy target? He couldn't help feeling that there was some underlying reason for speaking to him in this way and he realised he must be wary and exercise caution. There were more ways of robbing a man than hitting him on the head and knocking him to the ground.

The markets were large and crowded. Some of the stalls were manned by heavily tattooed mountain people wearing traditional hand woven clothes. There were sections selling meat and fish, fresh vegetables and marvellous looking strawberries. There were textiles, bags, brass ornaments, baskets, blankets, linen, brooms and woodcarvings of all kinds. Everywhere they walked Jamie was introduced to a brother, a sister, a cousin, an uncle. They shook his hands. They smiled at him. They welcomed him warmly. Whatever they could to help him, they would do willingly. All he needed to do was ask. He was overwhelmed by their kindness.

By now Jamie had been on his feet for two hours and Feli realised that he was exhausted. She offered to take him to her house, which was close by. He could sit there and rest for a while. She would make him tea to drink and when he had rested they could, perhaps, stroll through Burnham Park to look at the flowers and trees. She was sure he would find the park beautiful and peaceful after the busy turmoil of the markets. Marci would, of course, come with them.

The house was a primitive, one-roomed hovel and Jamie was appalled. He kept his reaction to himself, however, and gratefully accepted the offer of a chair to sit on. There was only one chair and, when the tea was made, Marci and Feli sat cross-legged on a covered mattress on the floor. Feli had to go outside to boil the water for the tea. There was no indoor bathroom or cooking area.

Although Marci was acting as a chaperone, she did nothing to prevent Jamie and Feli from exchanging frequent looks of longing and smiles of love. Every time Jamie caught Feli's eye she gazed at him with such intimacy and warmth that his stomach churned and his heart beat high with desire. As they walked slowly through Burnam Park, with its profusion of flowers and its beautiful boating lake, Jamie was overwhelmed by the need to touch Feli. Several times he allowed himself to brush up against her. When he did so she responded by pressing her arm or her leg against him, allowing the moment to last as long as possible before they separated to continue walking. He was sure that Marci observed what they were doing but she did nothing to stop them so they increased the frequency of their physical contact. Finally their bodies were so tantalisingly close that it was possible to touch almost all the time. Marci simply smiled to herself. Jamie could see that she was well pleased with the progress that he was making with Feli. It was quite clear that she approved of them establishing a relationship.

Within the next few days, Jamie could see that a concerted family effort was being made to trap him into marriage. The conspiracy was entirely lacking in subtlety. Family members would say, quite blatantly, 'Feli is a good, loyal girl. She would make an excellent wife.' And because they were all working so arduously to achieve this goal, Jamie became wary. How did Marci manage to spend so much time acting as a chaperone? It seemed to him that she had abandoned both her children and her job in order to enable Feli to spend as much time as possible in his presence. The family knew that Jamie's primary purpose in coming to the Philippines was to purchase merchandise for his market stall and they did all they could to arrange for his business concerns to be dealt with swiftly, presumably so that he would be free to concentrate on Feli. He was grateful for this because his concerns were actually in perfect accord with theirs. He wanted to be with Feli; he wanted to be with her every moment for the rest of his life but he didn't want her family to think that their efforts in this respect had anything to do with possible outcomes. He believed, in his heart, that Feli was sincere in her response to him but her family wanted a marriage so badly that he began to doubt and hesitate. He needed to be alone with Feli if he were going to come to any valid conclusion about her integrity. So far, being alone with her had been forbidden.

By the fourth day he'd had enough. He decided to confront Marci. 'Look, Marci, this is no good. I need time alone with Feli. I have to be able to talk to her without you being there. You inhibit both of us. Now what are we going to do about it?'

'I could sit in the lobby of the hotel while you take Feli into the restaurant for lunch. The cafeteria area is quite open. I could find a place where I'd be able to see you both, but you'd still be able to have a private conversation,' she said.

Jamie would have preferred to take Feli up to the privacy of his room. If he could hold her in his arms, caress her gently, touch her soft skin, her face, her hair then he'd be able to tell whether her response was genuine or not. But he knew Marci would never agree to that so he settled for lunch. The moment he had Feli to himself she swept away all his doubts.

'Forgive my family, Jamie. I tell them to stop but they take no notice of me. They do not believe that we are in love. They think they must help. They think you are a poor, crippled man who can be persuaded to marry a girl like me. They think that if they are very nice to you, if they treat you well and do everything they can for you, then you will see how good it would be for you to marry me. They do not understand that I looked into your face and I loved you and you looked into my face and you loved me. I do not see your crippled body. I see you.'

'Oh, Feli, I've waited all my life for a woman to say that to me. Are you sure, quite sure, that you love me? I don't think I could bear to be hurt by you.'

'Hurt you? I could never hurt you. I could only love you.'

'Then you will marry me? And come to Australia with me to live?' said Jamie.

'I'll go anywhere with you. Of course I want to come to Australia. Every Filipino girl has such a dream. But if you decided it would be better for you to come and live with me here, in the Philippines, I would be just as happy. I want to be with you forever. That's all.'

The family could relax after Jamie declared that he intended to marry Feli. They would have liked him to marry her immediately but they bowed to his decision that he would return in three months' time for the wedding. He needed to prepare his family for this momentous change in his life and to organise permission to bring Feli back to Australia with him. And Feli needed time to apply for a passport, to make the wedding arrangements, buy a bridal gown and purchase a few modest outfits suitable for a young woman coming to make Australia her home. Jamie would leave sufficient money to cover any costs that were entailed.

So now they had five or six days to spend together before it was time for Jamie to leave Baguio. Marci continued in her role as chaperone but was much more tolerant than she had been initially. She frequently left them alone for an hour or so, although she usually stayed within sight. Their relationship, therefore, remained chaste and pure but they talked about how wonderful it would be to touch, to kiss, to caress, to lie in one another's arms. They even plotted ways and means of evading Marci, hoping that they would be able to satisfy their desire to be truly alone together some time before Jamie's departure.

The three of them went sightseeing. They visited the Mountain Province Museum, the Philippine-Japanese Friendship Garden and the crystal caves. They took a half-day excursion to the Asin Hot Springs where Jamie paid for them to luxuriate in the hot sulphur baths. They went to Colorado Falls for a picnic and swam in the cool, deep, natural pool at the base of the falls. Jamie bought them lunch every day and paid for taxis to drive them out of the city, along scenic highways, stopping at vantage points to take photos of spectacular coastal views or to watch amazing sunsets.

He asked them to recommend a faith healer but he was disappointed in the experience. He expected some sort of charismatic spectacle but the healer they took him to see was a very ordinary looking man, working in a large, almost empty room in a suburban house. He asked Jamie to take off his shoes, his shirt and his trousers and to lie down on the small bed in the centre of the room. The man ran his hands over Jamie's gnarled joints, then took small squares of printed paper and placed them at strategic places all over Jamie's body. He began to pray and chant in some language that Jamie did not understand. He kept this up for twenty minutes or so, his hands constantly hovering just above the surface of Jamie's skin. When he'd finished, he removed the pieces of paper and told Jamie, in English, that he should not smoke or drink alcohol and that he should make sure that he gave his body plenty of rest. And that was that.

Afterwards Jamie complained. 'I thought faith healers were supposed to extract things from your body. That's what I saw on television. They performed operations without anaesthetics and they pulled out all this rotten, mucky stuff. They got rid of all the bad things that were inside their patients.'

'Those faith healers are only doing it for show,' said Feli. 'We took you to a real faith healer. Those papers he put on your body were direct prayers to God. He genuinely prayed for your recovery. God will listen to his prayers and you will feel better.' Jamie found that hard to believe but he didn't want to argue the point. He may not have found a cure for his illness in the Philippines but he'd found something far more valuable. He had found Feli. He had found love.

The day before he was due to leave, Marci said they could go up to Jamie's hotel room. She could not leave them alone in the room but she would sit in a chair by the window with her back turned to them. She would read a book. They could pretend that she was not there. They would be able to be more intimate with each other than had so far been possible because they would not be in a public place. No one would see them. He must not, however, allow anyone else in Feli's family to know that she had permitted them such an opportunity. If the family found out they would criticise her for being negligent in her role as chaperone. She felt sorry for them, that's all, and she trusted them. She knew that Jamie respected Feli and understood that, as a good Catholic girl, she must remain a virgin until her wedding night.

The hotel room was large with two single beds, a small table and two comfortable chairs. Marci took one of the chairs and moved it to a place in the room that was as far away as possible from the beds. She took out her book, sat down on the chair, crossed her legs and began to read. But was she really reading? They could see her shoulders and the back of her head. Jamie thought that, under similar conditions, he himself would find it impossible to read. She must be listening, or at least half listening to any sounds that he and Feli might make. He felt totally inhibited by her presence and was about to declare that this whole situation was ridiculous when Feli timidly took his hand and led him to the furthest single bed. She lay down and held her arms out to him. She drew him down beside her, placed her head on his chest and lay quite still beside him until she could feel his tension subside.

She lifted her face and turned towards him so that they could look into each other's eyes. Without making a sound, she mouthed the words, 'I love you' and lifted her lips to meet his. He expected her kiss to be cool and chaste but her breath was hot, her lips greedy with desire and she sighed with relief when, at last, their mouths came together. Marci's presence was an intolerable intrusion and, at first, he found it impossible to respond but Feli persisted. She continued to kiss him hungrily and, in between kisses, she touched his face, stroked his forehead, ran her fingers through his hair and smiled at him with such warm affection that he began to feel more comfortable.

In her passion she maintained both silence and control and he followed her lead, allowing himself to be guided to what she regarded as an appropriate level of desire. She would not allow his hands to wander down her body. She would not permit him to touch her breasts and although she was lying in his arms she rebuffed any effort he made to press his body closely against hers. He accepted the boundaries she established and found that he could let himself float on a gentle, exquisite, manageable level of desire. Soon he and Feli were locked into the silent world of their love for one another and Marci ceased to exist. It was something of a shock when, some considerable time later, Marci cleared her throat and said, 'In five minutes I'm going to turn around. We've been here for two hours. I think that's long enough.'

It was not long enough but it was all he was going to get and the memory of those two hours would have to sustain him for the next three months. Although leaving Feli was unbearable, part of Jamie was eager to go. The sooner he got home and sorted everything out the sooner he would be back to claim what he had always believed he deserved, the genuine love of a caring woman who was able to ignore his disabilities and love him for himself.

Jamie expected his father to express mild disapproval of his choice of a bride but he was unprepared for the vehement opposition thrown at him by both his parents. Walter's line of argument was predictable. 'Marry a girl from the Philippines? You must be mad. She doesn't love you. She just wants a passport to Australia. She'll dump you as soon as she gets Australian citizenship. Or she'll use you to get her whole damn family out here. We won't be supporting just your wife. We'll be overrun by dozens of relatives, all expecting handouts. It's out of the question. I'm not going to let you marry her. If you marry her then that's the end. You can't expect any more financial help from me, not ever.'

'I don't need your money. I can earn enough of my own. We're in love, I tell you. And I'm going to marry her, no matter what you say,' said Jamie.

It was his mother's reaction that he found hurtful. She was usually so supportive of any decisions he made but now she was behaving as if he had committed some crime. 'You can't bring her here. You're not going to bring a girl like that to live in my house,' said Elizabeth.

'A girl like what, Mum? She's a quiet, innocent, loving, sincere girl. When you meet her, you'll see. You'll get on well with her, I promise you.'

'I thought you'd have more sense, James. Those people over there are so poor they'll grab onto anyone to marry. She's using you. Can't you see that?' said Elizabeth.

'She loves me, Mum. I thought you'd be pleased that at last I've found someone who cares about me.'

'She can't love you,' said Elizabeth.

'Why not? Because no one could love a cripple like me? That's what you mean, isn't it?'

'You've been hurt so many times. I hate to think of you being hurt again,' said Elizabeth.

'Do you know what, Mum? I think you're jealous. I think you want to keep me to yourself. You've given so much of your life to looking after me that now, when I've really found someone who wants to take over from you, you can't bear to give up your role.'

'That's ridiculous, James,' said Elizabeth. 'You know there's nothing I want more in the world than for you to be independent and happy. But you will need looking after.'

'And you think you're the only one capable of doing that?' said Jamie.

'At least I do know what I'm capable of. I don't know anything about this girl of yours.'

'All you need to know,' said Jamie, 'is that I love Feli and she loves me. Her love is going to give me a new lease of life.'

The arguments continued over the next few months. Walter and Elizabeth maintained their opposition and made ugly threats in their attempt to get Jamie to change his mind. However, Jamie remained firm in his resolve. He had found love and no one was going to take it away from him. When they realised they could not influence him they grudgingly accepted the situation. Elizabeth said that he could, initially, bring Feli to live in the house and Walter said that he might buy Jamie a home of his own in a few years' time, if he could see that Feli was genuine in her affections.

Fighting with his parents exhausted Jamie's meagre supply of energy. He felt tired and ill and irritable. He kept himself going by writing to Feli every day and he was sustained by the short, sweet, simple letters of love that she managed to send him at least once a week. He appreciated her efforts because writing in English was obviously difficult for her. When she came to live with him he hoped to give her the opportunity to improve her education.

Applying for permission to bring Feli to Australia as his wife was time consuming but all arrangements were completed within the three months. On the day Jamie was due to return to the Philippines, Walter insisted on driving him to the airport. Jamie wished he'd called a taxi instead because his father did nothing but grumble and complain. Walter was having considerable trouble with pain in his right hip and lugging Jamie's suitcase from the car to the air terminal did not help his condition. By the time they reached the check-in counter they were so angry with one another that it was difficult to be civil.

'You're behaving like a fool, Jamie. You know that, don't you?' said Walter.

'And you're a failure as a father,' said Jamie. 'You've never made any attempt to know or understand me.'

'I only want what's best for you,' said Walter.

'I know what's best for me. Marrying Feli is the best thing in the world for me,' said Jamie. He turned away from his father and moved as quickly as he could towards the departure gate. He didn't bother to turn around and wave goodbye.

By the time the plane landed in Manila, Jamie felt ill. Something he'd eaten had given him severe indigestion and the burning in his chest was accompanied by waves of nausea. As soon as he reached his hotel, he lay down on the bed, deciding that he would make no attempt to go down to the hotel restaurant for dinner. He managed to get up a few hours later to have a shower and although the pain in his chest had not completely disappeared, it was certainly less severe. He thought he'd take some sleeping pills to make sure he had a restful night. Hopefully he'd feel well by morning.

When he woke next morning the pain was gone but he felt dizzy when he tried to get out of bed. Probably the effect of the sleeping pills. He might have taken too many. Another shower would solve the problem. Then he'd pack his things, go down for an early breakfast and be ready for his transfer to the airport. In three hours he'd be in Baguio. If he could just get there, and feel Feli's arms around him, then everything would be alright.

It was impossible to eat. A dull pain in the centre of his chest spread up his throat to his jaw and down along his left arm as soon as he entered the restaurant. The sight of the long tables, laden with buffet breakfast food was enough to nauseate him. Just get to the airport. Get on the plane. Get to Baguio. Get to Feli.

Dizziness. Nausea. Clammy hands. Trembling lips. Perhaps he had a fever. The flu. Food poisoning. He told his transfer driver that he was ill. Offered the man extra money to stay with him, look after him, see him safely onto the plane. The only thing to do. Couldn't have made it on his own.

Seated at last on the plane. An hour away from Baguio. An hour away from Feli. Pain subsiding. Then surging again, radiating across his chest. Angina. He knew perfectly well what it was but until this moment he had not allowed the word to enter his consciousness. 'Angina pectoris' to be more precise, caused by a lack of blood to the heart. But what did it mean? Now. At this moment. Would it pass? Or was it a warning, the precursor to an imminent heart attack? He had to be alright. He had to. No choice. He'd come all this way for a marriage and a marriage there was going to be. Feli! Feli! Her love would calm his clamouring heart and save him from disaster.

When the plane landed and taxied to a halt, Jamie tried to stand up but even the slightest exertion resulted in chest pain so he decided to wait until everyone else had left the plane before attempting to get up again. This time he succeeded and made his way into the terminal. He survived the passport check but felt too ill to collect his luggage. He'd just go out and find Feli. Worry about his luggage some other time. There she was. Standing behind the barrier. Waiting. Smiling. Waving. With two of her brothers. And cousin Marci. He staggered towards her. He willed himself to cover the distance that separated him from Feli's welcoming arms but he didn't quite make it. He collapsed on the floor at her feet.

An ambulance was called. They took him to hospital. Not the main city hospital but a small, mission hospital, high in the hills. Feli knew that this would be the right place for him to go. The nuns who ran the mission were kind and good. They'd put Jamie to rest in one of their cool, white, private rooms. They'd tend him with love and care. They'd make him well. In a few days' time he'd be rested, cured, ready for their wedding which was scheduled to take place one week from today. All would be well.

She stayed at his bedside. She held his hands. She whispered words of everlasting love. Every time he opened his eyes he saw her gentle face and he knew that her love for him was real and true. His heart seemed to be expanding inside his chest and he could feel that soon, very soon, there would be no space left to accommodate it. It would grow to such a monstrous size that it would explode inside him and then his pain would come to an end. He wanted to tell her that he loved her, that she had brought him joy and happiness, that she had given a measure of meaning to his short and painful life but he was quite incapable of speech. So he held her hand and waited. When his heart finally burst his body arched and his head was thrown back in a quick, sharp jerk. Some might have said that his lips curved in a twisted grimace of excruciating pain. But Feli did not think so. She was sure that she could see a smile hovering around Jamie's mouth.

Also available from Leone Sperling

COINS FOR THE FERRYMAN

ONE

She has come to visit me. Bundling, grey efficiency – severe-faced, square-jawed, high cheek-boned, rouged, slim-waisted, small-breasted, neatly packaged in round-necked, pastel-coloured, candy-striped dress – my mother.

It is Friday, 10am. Her eyes dart guarded glances at my untidy lounge room. The deep, soft, gold and maroon tapestry-patterned bean-bag chairs flop in comfortable disarray. I can almost discern, in their disordered curves, the imprint of the four little bodies that, last night, nested curled in their velvet warmth.

She looks around. Her hands itch. She picks up a doll with a vegemite face. She cannot hide her distaste. She longs to scream at me, wants to shout out her disgust, ask me how I can possibly live in such a filthy, unhygienic mess. She says nothing. She keeps herself in control. I want her to shout at me so that I can shout back at her. I want her to attack me so that I can defend myself. But in my family no one shouts. We keep our screams locked carefully below throat level. Our howls reverberate in our bellies. We never, never let them out.

'Would you like a cup of coffee?' I ask politely, showing that I know how to play the game, not allowing the aggressive 'What are you doing here? What do you want?' questions to rise any further than my navel.

She can't help it. While I'm putting on the kettle she has to gather the dirty breakfast dishes, scrape the greasy bits of bacon and half-eaten toast off the plates.

'I'll just wash up these few dishes, dear,' she says, 'while you're making the coffee.'

I want to tell her not to wash them up, but the words don't come out. I feel an angry scream mounting inside me but I squash it down and make a grab for a leftover piece of cold toast before it disappears into the rubbish bin. I half chew it and swallow it down quickly to keep the scream from surfacing.

'I thought I would come and give you a hand,' she says.

'I don't need any help,' I reply. Have I actually said the words? I'm not sure. Maybe they are just the words that I would like to be able to say. She goes on as if I haven't said them so I assume I've kept quiet.

'I thought,' she continues, 'that as you're going away on Sunday, you might need some help to get things cleaned up before you leave.'

'I don't need any help.' This time I'm damned sure I've said the words out loud, but she still goes on as if I haven't. I take the biggest apple I can see in the fruit bowl and tear off an enormous bite with my teeth. I keep chewing while she talks to me.

'You don't have it easy,' she says, you girls today. Not like my day. I always had a maid to help me. Look at you – divorced, alone with four children, a big house to run, a full-time teaching job. It's not easy, not easy at all.

I swallow my mouthful of apple and take a deep breath. I speak very loudly and very clearly. 'I don't need any help.' She looks hurt.

'Thanks very much for offering, Mum, but I can do it myself.' A year ago I couldn't have said it. A year ago I'd have let her bulldoze her way through our belongings and create order out of our chaos.

She sits down to drink her coffee. 'Well, dear,' she says, 'I'll just have a cup of coffee with you before I go.' I have defied her, but now some inner force compels me to open the biscuit cupboard. My hands take out the new packet of chocolate biscuits. My fingers tear off the cellophane wrapping and then from hand to mouth the biscuits go – shove, crunch, swallow.

She pretends not to notice what I'm doing in the hope of hiding her horror. She thinks that if she ignores what I'm doing then I'll stop doing it. She's wrong. I would like to be able to stop eating the chocolate biscuits but I don't know how to do that. She keeps on pretending that she's not watching me. But I know she's watching me and that makes it impossible for me to stop. She would like to grab hold of me and shake me and make me stop. She would like to scream, 'How can you be such a pig!' But she sticks to the rules, confining her scream to her eyes.

I think I'm going to vomit. I wish I would. But I know I won't. I never vomit. My stomach's made of elastic.

'You really need to get away, dear, don't you,' she says, sympathetically.

'Yes, I do,' I reply, struggling for control.

'You know, dear,' she goes on, trying not to count the exact number of biscuits I've eaten, 'when you get to London you must book yourself up on organized tours. Believe me, it's the only way to travel. That's what Daddy and I have found. Someone else does all the worrying for you. And you meet such nice people. People who speak your own language. I mean otherwise, dear, you might be very lonely, mightn't you, going overseas for six weeks all by yourself.'

I stare at her, through her. She goes on talking. I retreat. I don't know what she's talking about. Going overseas 'alone'. What does she mean? Doesn't she see that, on my life's journey, I am constantly accompanied by two grandmothers, three aunts, five cousins, one brother, one sister, one father, an ex-husband and four children? Above all, doesn't she realize that I always carry her iron-grey image around with me? Doesn't she understand that I'll be taking her overseas with me? Hopefully I'll lose her – somewhere along the way.

She leaves and I am alone with myself and my thoughts, my house and my mess to puddle and muddle and sift through and order. And I do it, in my own quiet, chaotic way. By the end of the day I have achieved a semblance of order that my children would regard as tolerable. If the dining room table is still piled high with the favourite possessions of four small people, then who cares? We never eat at the dining room table anyway. To the five of us, our mess connotes warmth, love, friendliness. Why should we care if it offends the eye of the outsider? We are snug and warm and secure in our sea of dolls and cars and guns and books and sticky, soft caresses.

My eyes fill with tears. I allow the trickling warmth to tumble down my cheeks. Can I bear to leave them, to be separate from them, for six whole weeks? How will they manage without me? I'm forty years old. Time, surely, to go off on my own for a while – to have a look at the world, to have a look at myself. Of course they can manage without me.

Time, too, I realize, to pick them up from school. It is the last dreary day before the long summer holidays begin. My three sons come bounding out of the gate. How little it takes to make their eyes shine – a hailstorm, a rainbow, an ice cream, the last day of school. I try to look at them objectively and can't. Surely anyone would find them beautiful. The oldest boy – large, placid, responsible, almond-eyed. The second – little, nuggety, tough, aggressive, black cherry eyes. The third – precious, gentle, sensitive, blonde-curled, soft-lipped. They all want to talk at once. It's impossible. I shout for silence, allot turns (youngest first) and each boy's news bubbles out. They are all high on holidays.

We pick up the littlest one. She is waiting anxiously. Tiny, exotic, dark-haired, delicate girl-child. I pick her up and hug her and feel her little arms about my neck. She tolerates my show of affection because she hasn't seen me all day. We bundle into the car and they talk excitedly of holidays and fun, of beaches and picnics, of films they want to see, of Christmas Day at Grandma's house, of presents they might get. Suddenly someone mentions the fact that I will not be there. An appalling silence descends upon us all.

* * * * *

'I understand,' she says, with absolute assurance, 'that you need to be on your own for a while. When I grow up, she goes on, 'I'll want to be alone for a while too.'

It is Sunday. 10am. The day I am due to leave on the grand world tour. She is sitting up on the bench next to me, while I wash up the breakfast dishes. She is six years old.

I don't know what to say to her.

'Will it upset you,' I ask, 'to stay with Grandma and with Daddy while I'm away?'

'Not at all,' she replies. She goes on, 'It's perfectly natural for you to want to be alone. You might,' she adds, 'even write some more stories while you're away.' I want to dry my hands, hug her, kiss her, tell her I love her, tell her it's not her I want to leave, tell her she must know how much I love her, explain to her that its just that I need to be alone for a while, need to sort myself out, see where I'm going. But she's not asking me for reassurance, she's not begging for love, so I can't give it to her.

I go on washing-up and I listen to the chatter.

Why is she so secure and why am I so insecure? My mother's words on the telephone half an hour ago still echo in my ears – 'Not coming to the airport … such a hot day …you don't mind, do you dear? …such big crowds … not coming to say goodbye.' I am shocked numb. I cannot believe she will not come.

I finish in the kitchen and go into my bedroom to pack my suitcase. I know exactly what I'm taking so it's not a difficult task to carry out. While I'm packing my mind goes back to yesterday.

It is Saturday. 1pm. It's my last full day with the children and I want them to be happy. 'Take us to Luna Park!' they all beg and plead. I hate Luna Park. I always refuse to take them there. I must be feeling terribly guilty about going away without them because I find myself agreeing to take them. They are unbelievably ecstatic.

As soon as we get there, they make me go on some dreadful machine that twirls me into space. I am quite sure I'm going to die. I can't even open up my eyes. They laugh at my terror. They get more pleasure from my fear than they do from the monstrous contraption we're riding on. I realize how afraid I am to leave the face of Mother Earth. Yet my children can leave it with defiant laughter, positive that no harm will come to them.

They make me go on the Ferris wheel. I'm not too bad while it's moving, but it keeps stopping to let more people on. Every time it stops I feel an overwhelming urge to jump off and smash myself on the ground below. I cling on to the two littlest children as if their tiny hands can hold my compulsion down.

They look at my terror. They shriek delightedly to each other, 'Look at Mummy! She's so scared she has to hold on to us. Look at her! Look at her!'

'Don't move!' I yell at them. 'Don't move! You'll fall!' They are doubled up with laughter. The more they laugh the more they move. The more they move the more terrified I become. I see all five of us – a mound of indecipherable arms and legs, blood, flesh, brains emptying onto the pavement.

Thank God! It's not going to stop any more – it's going to keep moving. We just might survive after all. I find it's alright when the wheel is coming downwards towards the ground but when I am drawn upwards, away from the earth, my entire being shrieks a silent protest. The ride ends. They have to help me off. I am totally disordered. They sit me down. Their laughter turns to concern. They fuss over me. 'Are you alright, Mum?' 'Do you feel sick?' 'Can I get you a drink?' I am so shattered I cannot even reply. This is ridiculous. I don't want to frighten them. This is their day. We are all supposed to be having fun. With enormous effort I pull myself back to them. I laugh at myself. 'What a stupid mother I am, to be so afraid of heights.'

They are reassured. They like me to see myself in the role of 'stupid mother'. It makes them feel more grown up. I send them off with a few dollars to buy themselves ice creams while I get on quietly with the process of knitting myself together again. By the time they get back I'm all in one piece.

I've been 'good' so far today. Being 'good' means eating healthy foods, like meat and eggs and fruit and vegetables. Being 'good' means eating no bread and no cakes and no sweets and no chocolate biscuits. I've found, to my great surprise, that there's a health food shop at Luna Park. You can actually buy yoghurt instead of hot-dogs and fairy-floss. I'm pleased with myself for having been 'good' today.

My daughter suddenly hands me a sticky, dripping ice cream. 'I've had enough,' she says. Its melting sweetness is inside my mouth before I realize what's happened. One mouthful is all it needs for me to lose the battle for the day. For the rest of the afternoon I join the children on an endless orgy or waffles, ice cream, hot chips, soft drinks, lollies and fairy-floss until we all stagger to the car. They are full, warmly satisfied. A great day. I am bloated with despair. If I cannot cope with a Ferris wheel, how the hell am I going to cope with a jumbo jet?

I come back to my bedroom and my packing and to the two biggest boys bursting into my room, asking me how much money I'll give them to spend at the airport.

They are so calm. They behave as if today were any ordinary day. I feed on their tranquility and realize that they are quite able to let me go. They know I'll come back. They know that our circle of loving will always be there – warm, complete, secure.

How I wish I could be like them, but my mother's words are still banging away there inside my head – 'Not coming to the airport' – and I am forced to face the extraordinary truth that not one of my children is bound to me as I am bound to her.

They help me put my things in the car and we go off for our final treat. We are going to a Chinese restaurant for lunch and afterwards to the airport. My plane is due to leave at 4pm.

They love Chinese food and I don't mind taking them because it's always possible to be 'good' at a Chinese restaurant. I'm happy to stick to meat and vegetable dishes. Not like McDonald's. That's a nightmare. At McDonald's I am constantly faced with the temptation of Big Macs and French fries and ice cream sundaes with hot caramel sauce. At a Chinese restaurant I feel reasonably safe.

I'm very on edge. Anxiety. Terror. Anticipation. I remind myself, between the vegetable soup and the beef chop suey, that I've never been on my own for any sustained period of time. I have gone from belonging to belonging; from school to university to marriage; from parental home to marital home; from being a child to being a wife to being a mother. There has never been a time when I have been responsible only to myself, belonged only to myself.

I feel that I ought to reprimand my third son, who is eight years old, for shoveling beef and oyster sauce into his mouth with a spoon and a hand instead of with a spoon and a fork. I stop myself. He is having such a marvelous time, gravy all over his hands and face. The frequent reprimands of my children's father momentarily disturb me, almost prompt me to tell my son to use his fork. 'Why can't you teach them some table manners! They can't even use a knife and fork properly.' He's right. They do embarrass him when he takes them out. But if I do reprimand my son it will be with his father's voice, not my own. He's not embarrassing me. I don't give a damn. I just enjoy watching his total immersion in messy pleasure. I win over the father's voice. I say nothing to my son. No! Damn it! I haven't won at all because suddenly I'm asking my daughter if she really wants all the rice she's ordered and she gives me some and before I know it I'm shoving rice into my mouth. Now I know for certain that when I buy them an ice-block after the Chinese meal, I'll have to buy one for myself as well. They'll be satisfied with water ice-blocks. I'm going to need an ice cream, probably with chocolate coating. I sink into despair. I am nothing but my mouth. I fuse with the food. I am the food. I cannot distinguish the boundaries of my self. I cease to exist. The avalanching, rumbling monster in my belly asserts himself again.

I try to picture him. He is a lion, roaring there in the dark hollow of my insides, demanding his right to gobble people up. I don't want him to gobble people up and, above all, I don't want anyone to know that he's inside me so I keep throwing him chunks of food to keep him quiet. I know I have to come to terms with him. If he and I are both going to inhabit this body for the rest of its life then we're going to have to understand each other. It seems to me that I'm always considerate about his needs but he doesn't make much effort to understand mine. At times I've thought of trying to exorcise him. But if I got him out of myself what would be left? How would I fill the gaping hole he left behind? Would there be anything left? Or am I synonymous with my lion; are he and I one entity and if I let him die would I die too? I don't know. So I keep on feeding him – just in case.

Am I mad? I don't really know but I don't think so. It all makes sense to me. I am born under the star of Leo and I carry my sign within me. A few times I've tried to tell people about it but when I do so I sense that they think what I'm saying is peculiar so I've learned to keep quiet about it, most of the time.

I don't just buy them ice-blocks. I become generous. I let them buy peppermint creams and thin, round, dark-chocolate discs from the expensive sweet shop that is just over the road from the Chinese restaurant. They can't believe their luck but my generosity is deceptive. I'm being cunning. I know that this shop sells mouth-watering Turkish Delight. My stomach is full but there is no connection between hunger and my need to eat. I have to have the sweet. I buy a whole pound. It's terribly rich. Any normal person would be satisfied with one or two pieces. I eat the lot. In five minutes it's all gone.

I want to vomit. I long to vomit. The rich, sticky sweetness nauseates me. I feel five months pregnant, my stomach distended and sore. I berate myself. 'You disgusting gluttonous pig,' I say to myself. I become the Turkish Delight, quivering, jelly-fat. I hate myself. I long for the day to be over. Tomorrow will be a new day, a new start, a new chance.

I always long for the magic of Mondays, a new beginning of a new week and if the first of the month happens to fall on a Monday then it seems to me that I have a double chance to start anew, to be 'good'. Maybe, just maybe, I will have the strength to get through a whole week, even a whole month, without stuffing myself with food. It never happens, of course. I'm so anxious about it being Monday that I'm usually shoveling food into myself by mid-morning.

I went to a hypnotist once. He stopped me from smoking and I thought he might be able to stop me from eating. It didn't work though. Sometimes, for no apparent reason, it goes away for a while and I actually stay on a diet for months and months. I get really slim and as soon as that happens I start eating again and put on all the weight I've lost. I once told myself that if it hadn't gone away by the time I was forty I'd kill myself. I'm forty now and it hasn't gone away. I can't very well kill myself though, can I? I've got four children relying on me.

And it happened again last night. It hasn't happened for years. I had a dream. People kept coming into my room, lots of people – my brother, my sister, Mum and Dad, men I've known. They held up a big white sheet next to my bed or maybe it was a flag – yes, that's right – an American flag or a Union Jack. I thought they might wrap me up in it. Perhaps it was my shroud. But they didn't. They just held it up so that I couldn't see behind it. I heard noises, though. I knew they were all screwing behind that flag and I was all alone; no one was making love to me and I felt so lonely that I started to cry and suddenly I couldn't breathe – I was choking, choking, choking and I woke up and I was suffocating, my face squashed in the pillow and I had to use every bit of strength I've got to force myself up on to my arms, to get my face out of the pillow that was smothering me, suffocating me, killing me. I was wide awake then, wet, shaking. I'll die that way. One day I'll dream my suffocating dream and it will really happen. I know that's the way I'll go back.

I've dreamed similar dreams ever since I can remember. At one time it frightened me so much that I wouldn't go to sleep. I was eighteen years old. I was sure I was going to die if I let myself go to sleep. She had to sit on my bed and keep me calm until I fell asleep. Like a mother should - for her baby.

She thinks I've forgotten but I haven't. I remember being born. No one believes me when I say that so it's another thing I've learned to keep quiet about. But I do remember. I remember before I was born too. I remember swimming soft in the sunlight of the womb, rocked gentle, lulled, swaying in her belly. I remember that I preferred to breathe through our chord, our harmony of food and air, complete and total flow. I never wanted to be born at all. She and I – so separate, so remote, so far from understanding each other; she and I were one once, tuned in to each other's needs. I moved when she moved, stopped when she stopped, started with fright at her fears, cried when she cried, laughed when she laughed. Fused together.

No wonder I resisted her efforts to expel me. I could not understand why I shouldn't stay in there forever. She'd been quite happy about our union for nine months, why did she now jerk and move the walls of my fortress, make them hard and rigid, drain away my soft fluid bed? Dry and harsh she became, forcing me movement by movement down her hostile canal, muscles contracting upon me, pushing, pushing, pushing me out into the stabbing air, the bright-lit sterility. And in her haste to rid herself of me she didn't even notice that she'd let the cord wind itself around my neck so that the moment of my birth was fired with harsh, rasping, choking strangulation. Life and death mingled at my cold awakening on that bleak August day.

When I was a child I often dreamed of being chased and strangled by a long pink snake lady. It was not so much the chase that frightened me, not even the strangulation. What frightened me was the end of the dream, the moment when I realized that the face of the snake lady was exactly the same as the face of my mother.

* * * * *

I am at the airport. Sunday 3pm. I feel so separate from myself that for a moment I can't understand what on earth I'm doing here. They want money for lollies, drinks, to play the games on the machines. I keep doling it out. I don't care what it costs, as long as they are happy, as long as they don't cry. Please, God, if you exist don't let them cry.

I go to the check-in counter. It's a sweltering day. My clothes are wet. I have to carry a heavy sheepskin coat. Suddenly I remember a dream I had a few nights ago. In my dream I was standing, just as I am now, waiting to check in before boarding the plane. In my dream it was terribly hot, just as it is today. In my dream they called out our flight number and then read out the London weather report – 'Sleet, snow, temperatures below zero, freezing, rain.' I looked down at my clothes and saw that I was wearing a thin cotton dress and realized, at the same moment, that I had left my sheepskin coat at home. 'I've forgotten my coat. I've got to go home and get my coat!' Although I shouted and screamed I was locked in the crowd and they carried me, coatless, onto the plane. I felt the terror of knowing that when I reached London I would inevitably freeze to death.

The shock of the dream shivers through me and despite the heatwave conditions I clutch my sheepskin coat fiercely to me.

I am at the head of the check-in queue. My hand wets the plastic folder that holds my ticket, passport, traveller's cheques.

'Ticket please,' she says. I give her my ticket. I am very neurotic about my passport. I hope she won't ask for it. The reason I'm so neurotic about my passport is that I went through such trauma to acquire it. The red tape involved in digging up certified copies of marriage and divorce papers was bad enough. So was the implied insult from the Officer in the Immigration Department who felt that no adult lady could possibly be only 143 centimetres in height. But, worst of all, was my trip to the Registrar General's Department where my request for a copy of my birth certificate was met with the extraordinary reply that my birth had never been registered.

'It has to be there,' I told them. They checked again. There is a record of my older brother's birth; there is a record of my younger sister's birth. I feel negated. Wiped out. Why did they forget to register my birth? I ask them why. They say to each other:

'I thought you did it, Mummy dear.'

'No, dear, it was always your job to register the births.'

'Where do you want to sit,' she asks, 'aisle or window seat?'
I am about to say I don't care when my friend interrupts. He
has come to the airport to say goodbye to me and to take my
children back to their father's house. He has had a premonition
that my plane will crash.

'She'll sit right at the back of the plane,' he interjects, 'in
the last row.' He doesn't want me to go. He thinks he loves me.
He thinks I'll screw ten different men every day. He thinks I'll
forget him. He might be right. So he's invented the idea that
my plane will crash. The certain knowledge of my death has
come to him in a dream. He's had other dreams like this before.
They always come true. Normally such foreboding would ter-
rify me, but this time it doesn't. I tell him again that the plane
won't crash and that I refuse to die. I'm not sure that I believe
what I'm saying but by now I feel swept along too far to turn
back. I've got a real sense of inevitability right now. I just know
that I am going to get on that plane and go.

My third little boy flings himself into my arms and has
started to give me the 10,174 kisses that he has calculated he
will require to see him through the next six weeks. He is the
only one I am worried about. He seems to need me so much.
I know the others are self-assured enough to cope. We peck
at each other, little mouth kisses, lip to lip, endlessly building
his fortress of love. I suddenly wonder how he'll manage to
shit while I'm away. He has some anxiety about shitting. He
never does it at school or at anyone else's place. He always
waits for me. 'Start me off,' he says. That means I have to stand
at the toilet door while he starts. After the first 'plop' he's safe
and tells me I can go away. Can he go for six weeks without
a shit? I don't suppose he can. It's better than it used to be. I

used to have to sit on the floor outside the toilet and talk to him the whole time.

Sometimes he develops a compulsive sniff, or his eyes twitch, or he looks at the palms of his hands and then at the soles of his feet. The symptoms are always on the move. He never sticks to any of them for too long. And he can't drink any soft drink if anyone else has drunk out of the bottle and he can't eat his dinner if anyone else breathes on it. And, above all, he can't bear to look at straight arms. No one in the family is allowed to hold their arms out straight. I don't know why. But we all understand about his little peculiarities and he has managed to carve out for himself an area of tolerance that is given to no one else in the family. He gets migraines, too, but we all ignore them. He just lies upside down on the big bean-bag chair and falls asleep and he's all better in an hour or two. I've asked the other kids to look after him but will the adults who mind him understand? He lives on some other level of reality. He just visits us occasionally but whenever he comes to call he needs so much reassurance and love before he flits off again to his own, more interesting, realm of existence.

We're up to kiss number 764 when I suddenly hug him to me. Precious, curly-haired, ageless child. 'You'll be alright, won't you?' I ask fiercely.

'Seven-hundred-and-sixty-five, seven-hundred-and-sixty-six,' he goes on, unable to be distracted from his compulsive counting.

Everything to him is a matter of numbers. As soon as he meets someone he wants to know how old they are. He's not being rude. He just needs a new jumping off point for his end-less calculations. The patter goes something like this: 'If you're twenty-four years old then you're three times as old as I am and you're fifty-two years younger than Grandpa and sixteen years younger than Mummy. You might think I'll never be half your age but when you're thirty-two, I'll be sixteen and then I'll be half as old as you are.' It doesn't stop there. It goes on and on. At first you feel some need to check his calculations. Then you realize you're not supposed to do that. There's no doubt that he's right. You just have to keep nodding your head and mumbling, 'Yes'. He can't read very well and when he writes he holds his pencil in such a peculiar way that his letters emerge on the page as a spidery code of hieroglyphics. He thinks he isn't clever. I suspect he's a genius. We are up to kiss number 801. I go on and on because that's what he needs and I resist the desire to crush my warmth and my love into his little body.

'That'll do,' he says. 'I don't need as many as I thought I did.' I am relieved. I have visions of myself not being able to board the plane because we have not reached the magical number that will set him free.

My friend stands beside me, bleak. As my flight number is called he hugs me to him and I feel his tears on my cheek. Then I start to cry and I am bewildered. The children do not cry and they do not understand why we do. I have been so worried that they would be the ones to break down and now the sight of this adult crying absolutely undoes me. I break away from him and give my children a final hug. The two smallest ones are silent. I sense their state of shock. 'Have a good time,' the two big ones say, almost in unison, embarrassed by my tears.

I look at her, the littlest. In her tense eyes I see the wish to rush after me. She grabs her biggest brother's hand. He helps her hold herself back. She would like to spring from the crowd of people and dive into the plane with me. My last sight is of her tiny face, lips firmly pressed, holding back. I can't risk turning around. I dare not look at them again.

COINS FOR THE FERRYMAN
is available for Kindle, iBooks and POD at

www.cilentopublishing.com

AUTHOR'S BIOGRAPHY

Leone Sperling was born in Sydney in 1937, attended Sydney Girls' High School and graduated from Sydney University with a BA Honours degree in English literature. She taught English full-time with the NSW Department of TAFE for twenty years, a career that she found rewarding and fulfilling. She regards the fact that she did find time to write as a minor miracle because her marriage ended when her children were very young.

Three books, Coins for the Ferryman, Mother's Day and Oasis were published between 1981 and 1990. She was awarded a Literature Board grant in 1985. She has also had several short stories and articles published in national newspapers and Australian anthologies. These are now collected in The Book of Life.

After taking early retirement she wrote two novels, What About Love? and Jamie. She then undertook a four-year naturopathic Diploma in Nutrition. Leone now enjoys close, mutually rewarding relationships with her four children and six grandchildren and studies Latin with Continuing Education at Sydney University. Severe hearing impairment has resulted in the need for a Cochlear implant. For several years Leone has been on the Management Committee of Better Hearing Australia's Sydney branch and spends a considerable amount of time as a research volunteer with Cochlear and with the National Acoustic Laboratories.

Leone's writing is open and honest. Her style is spare and simple but constantly displays a willingness to confront and examine both the joyful and the darker aspects of human emotions and relationships.

www.ingramcontent.com/pod-product-compliance
Lightning Source LLC
Chambersburg PA
CBHW060435180626
46817CB00007B/2821